Noel McBride

Noel McBride

INKING

IN THE

OUTLINES

HALDEL

Published by HALDEL Publications 2013

Versions of some of these stories have appeared in other publications and been broadcast on radio.

ISBN: 978-0-9576487-0-8

Printed by Plantation Press

For Jean

In the probability this will never happen again I would like to thank my wife, Jean, who got me into writing in the first place (by paying my membership fee into a writing class!); my daughters, Deborah and Catherine, always supportive; my brother, George, and sister-in-law, Doreen, for their encouragement over the years; the members of Ards Writers, great people all, for their constructive criticism and camaraderie of a Tuesday night, David Torrans of No Alibis Bookstore and all those others who helped in various ways.

…And in memory of my mother and father and my brother, John.

Each had his past shut in him like the leaves of a book known to him by heart; and his friends could only read the title.

Virginia Woolf
Jacob's Room

Noel McBride was born and still lives in Belfast. He does not hold a degree in metaphysics. He has not, in his time, worked, variously, as a binman, coffin polisher, bouncer in a nightclub nor (perish the thought) been a male model for an art class. He has never climbed the north face of the Eiger (he has trouble climbing to the top deck of the number 4A bus) nor paddled up the Orinoco in a canoe. He does however confess to single-handedly disabling the lift mechanism in an office block in central Belfast (from inside the lift!) He is the same age as Cliff Richard but refuses to dye what remains of his hair and considers himself the better singer.

CONTENTS

HENRY MCCOMISKEY RIDES AGAIN

Henry McComiskey stood in the middle of the aisle, cereals on his right, mineral water to his left. Must be nearly forty years, he thought. He turned to face back towards the entrance and looked up, expecting to see the underside of the balcony. But there wasn't a balcony anymore. You could make out where the wall had been re-plastered after it had been removed and, if you stepped back far enough, the patches where the apertures into the projection room used to be. Downright shame, he thought, they could at least have kept those. He remembered as a boy wetting his half-ticket, wadding it into a ball and throwing it up into the projector's beam, watching its shadow arc across the screen.

On a point of principle Henry hadn't shopped there before. But the choice had been taken out of his hands when a plumber's apprentice, called in by Wondermac to repair a pipe, left his blowlamp beside the firelighter stock and burnt the building to the ground a week ago last Friday. Henry wondered which brand of firelighters they were as he had been having a bit of bother recently with his Baxi.

He strolled along the aisle, past the displays, expecting to find himself moving downwards but the floor didn't slope anymore either. Ahead of him, where the screen used to be was a plain beige wall. He stopped, looked up trying to visualise the way it had been. At first the images wouldn't come, but a piece at a time, as he stared at the blank wall, and starting with the smell of chewing gum and Jeye's fluid, the memories flooded back…

It's Saturday afternoon and Henry McComiskey is nine years old. This week it's Johnny Mack Brown in a three-reeler, only old Albert, the projectionist, is drunk again and we're seeing reel three instead of reel two. As a consequence, Johnny Mack Brown's left arm is in a sling and nobody knows why. Nobody seems to care much either, for three minutes ago somebody started to sing The Sash My Father Wore *to which someone responded with* The Soldier's Song *and each persuasion is now in full voice trying to drown out the other.*

Henry is a quiet child. He loves the films, especially those in black and white. He finds comfort in the fact that a black and white world is not a real world. Blood, on the rare occasion you see it, is black as distinct from bright, spurting Tarantino red.

Last week it was The Durango Kid. *Now there was a quick-change act if ever you saw one. At the first sign of a runaway stagecoach, the Kid had his horse, his* white *horse, round behind the nearest rock, re-emerging seconds later at the other end, a complete change of clothes, on a* black *horse eat your heart out Paul Daniels…*

…Henry is thirteen and it's five minutes to noon and Gary Cooper walks the street alone and afraid. Henry can't take his eyes off the screen, heart racing, but the film is black and white and he knows everything will turn out okay and when he gets home there'll be chips for tea…

"Excuse me, hmm – you wouldn't have change of a ten-pound note, would you?"

Henry's daydream ended abruptly. A little man stood there, all of five feet tall, in an old raincoat, green-checked cap, three-day stubble.

Henry shook his head. "Sorry – I haven't."

"Oh, dear." A look of despair came over the little man's face. "I don't have a pound coin…for the shopping trolley." He looked round him. "You wouldn't…you couldn't… by any chance…lend me, hmm…"

Henry rummaged in his pocket and handed over a pound coin.

"Oh, thank you ever so much, hmm. Very kind of you…I'll see you get it back immediately I empty the trolley, hmm …Very kind of you." He touched his cap brim and shuffled away but, instead of making for the trolley park, disappeared round the end of the chilled food cabinets.

Henry shrugged, picked up a packet of marshmallows, put them back again. Resist – got to lose a bit of weight, he'd found it a little difficult lately pulling on his socks.

Saturday matinees. Those were the days, eh? – Tex Williams, Rod Cameron, Wild Bill Elliott…and that other guy, whatsisname? – guy with the whip…dressed all in black…funny name.

He rounded the end of the aisle. Ahead of him the little man stood, hand outstretched, a young woman in a tracksuit dropping something into it. The little man touched the peak of his cap and backed away, profuse in his thanks.

Wee chancer, thought Henry, I should have known, resigning himself to the fact his pound coin was gone forever.

He turned, bumping into a rack of DVDs. He adjusted his glasses and fingered through them – Terminator 2, Reservoir Dogs, Judge Dredd – violence the common denominator. Among them were some special offers – Police Academy 4, Serpico, Bull Durham and, towards the back, Angel And The Badman…

…Henry is seventeen years old and grappling in the back row with Sally Palmer, six months older and built for comfort. He can't believe his luck. He hasn't a clue what has happened in the past ten minutes of the film – something about a wounded gunman nursed back to health by a dewy-eyed Quaker girl. The film is an old one on a re-run and most people have seen it before but it endures and the cinema is full…

Henry sighed, dropped a tin of peas into his basket. Sally Palmer. I wonder what became of her. The last he heard she'd run off with a sailor from Murmansk following promises of a sealskin coat and a secure job in a whalemeat factory.

There was knocking noise. Somewhere in the next aisle. Through a gap in the shelving he could see a green-checked cap. He walked to the end and peeped round. A large plastic bin occupied the middle of the aisle, a notice on the side: *Damaged tins half price*. Henry saw the little man lift a tin of fruit from the display and bang it gently against the shelf then drop it into a basket before shuffling quickly away.

Guy with the whip – What was his name? Henry could see him clearly now, the whip snaking out, wrapping itself round the baddie's gun hand, the gun dropping, then, the ultimate indignity – the laughter as the whip snipped through his belt, his trousers falling round his ankles.

Started with L, the name. Henry lifted a tin of pineapple chunks. Larry…Leslie …Lionel…Lionel? – Whoever heard of a cowboy called Lionel? Come to think of it, whoever heard of a cowboy called Marion? Need to be tough, a name like that.

The little man was standing now at the washing powders. He was fumbling at something and as Henry drew level he returned a packet to the shelf and lifted one beside it before moving away.

Henry glanced at the packets. He couldn't figure it out at first but then he noticed the top had been torn off one. He looked at the others. The tops all displayed an offer – *Ten pence off your next purchase with this coupon.*

L is for…Leroy. Was it Leroy?

The scream came from the direction of the checkout. Henry turned. The woman in the tracksuit was standing there, hands to her cheeks. The checkout girl, big girl in a bodywarmer, was on her feet facing a figure in a navy anorak, a balaclava hiding his face. He was pointing a gun, his hand unsteady. He shouted something at her but it was clear she wasn't going to cooperate.

Henry had a clear view of it all and the gunman was getting more unstable by the second.

Henry was standing beside the household hardware. He looked round him and picked up a brush shaft. He began to walk slowly, purposefully, up behind the gunman. The checkout girl was the first to see him, her face changing to a look of horror. "No!" she shouted at Henry. "No!"

The gunman spun round, pointed the gun at Henry, his hand shaking badly now. "Back!" he yelled. "Get back!"

But Henry kept on coming. The gunman waved the weapon again. "I'm warning you! I'm going to shoot!"

Henry was only feet away now. He stopped, the checkout girl gave a sigh of relief – and that was when Henry remembered. He looked down at the brush shaft. Of course, he thought. Of course!

The gunman was turning back towards the checkout. Henry raised the brush shaft above his head. *"GERONIMO!"* he yelled and charged.

The gunman spun back, the gun coming up. Henry lunged with the brush shaft and at the same time the checkout girl swung her hand round catching the man behind the ear with a tin of creamed rice. There was a loud bang and Henry felt something punch him in the chest, throwing him backwards.

He crashed into the rack behind him, dislodging a stack of magazines and slid down to a reclining position. All of a sudden he didn't feel very well. He tried to reach out to tidy the magazines but something was badly wrong. He coughed and his chest hurt. He thought he would just rest for a minute.

A gnarled hand appeared, holding something – a packet of paracetemol. "Here – take one of these, hmm. It'll make you feel better… Dearie me – you'll have a job getting that stain out."

Henry looked down. The front of his jacket was bright red. He touched it and his fingers came away wet. He was finding it hard to breathe. But it's not supposed to be this way… It's not supposed to be like this.

"Don't move, mister – Try not to move." A girl, seventeen or so, in a school uniform, knelt beside him. Beyond her the gunman was lying on the floor, pinned down by the checkout girl's ample bottom and she was yanking at the balaclava. It was coming off with difficulty and the way she was pulling there was every possibility his ears would as well. Henry thought; phew, I'm glad that's not me.

He started to slide sideways and the young girl slipped her arm round him. He felt cold. "Hold on," the girl said. "Hold on – there's an ambulance on the way."

Then another voice, a man; "It looks bad."

…Henry is in the back stalls, arm round Sally Palmer. John Wayne is sitting on the low back of a wagon cradling the dewy-eyed girl. "Not me, mister," he says – "From now on I'm a farmer." And the wagon moves off and the music builds and the lights are coming up and Sally is murmuring something in his ear and he turns to her and someone is tugging his arm and he doesn't want to go…

Henry opened his eyes. He felt himself being lifted…cold air, flashing lights, a sliding sensation, a girl, a different one now, leaning over him. She gently brushed his hair from his forehead, her hand cool. Something being pressed against his chest.

Voices now in the background; "Man's a hero – went for the guy with a brush shaft. Might as well have charged him with a balloon on a stick." And, then, at the ambulance door, another voice; "I don't suppose you're going anywhere near Primrose Street, hmm?"

A beeping noise now, somewhere near his head. A door closing. He pulled weakly at the girl's sleeve. What he had to say was important. The girl leaned over him but Henry had difficulty forming the words, then; "Tell me…" It was little more than a whisper… "Tell me…Whatever happened to Lash LaRue?"

The girl squeezed his hand. "Just lie still, sir – It won't be very long."

It was nice lying there with her holding his hand. She looked so serious that Henry wondered if he should enquire but decided to mind his own business so he just nodded. He could hear the sound of a siren. Must be something up, he thought. He was feeling quite sleepy and started to yawn and although he tried to stifle it he eventually had to give in. He hoped the girl wouldn't think he was being rude.

In a while he closed his eyes, his thoughts filled with canyons and cattle drives, sagebrush and tumbleweed and in the monochrome of his dreams he walked in the company of heroes.

INKING IN THE OUTLINES

Belfast, 1982

He stood, back against the door, conscious of the contrast between the street sounds of a moment ago and the stillness of the room – cold, musty-smelling. Should have lit the occasional fire, he thought. No point now. Anyway, all he'd wanted to do was get in, check round and get out again. Stupid even thinking that way.

He still hadn't moved. He looked round, hesitating when his eyes reached the meter box in the corner beside the window… Check the meter reading before you leave.

He looked at the patterned curtains, a colour match for the carpet – the only remaining items of furnishing in the house – and the fifties Devon fire surround. He smiled to himself; God, people were now paying a lot of money for an Adam and we had one pulled out.

He remembered the day the Devon was installed – midwinter like now and no fire for three days while the cement set, the newly-plastered chimney-breast providing the perfect surface for the graffiti contest with his brothers. And later, the minister calling one night, sitting, chair drawn up to the fire, chuckling at the drawings and limericks in front of him.

When he had redecorated for her a couple of years ago they were all still there, faded by time.

He turned quickly to where she used to sit and looked at…nothing.

He closed his eyes and pictured her sitting on the rocker beside the fire, talking, laughing, his father on the chair opposite, reading the paper. She had always been pleased when anyone called. Hardly through the door but she was up and putting on the kettle, bustling about in the tiny scullery, barely room to turn round, until he and his brother knocked down the wall separating it from the small back room, giving her the proper kitchen she had always wanted.

When the furniture comes out it fairly makes a difference, he thought. Looks a little shabby now – like there, where the back of the settee has rubbed against the wallpaper…and there, the marks where the pictures and mirror used to hang.

He moved through into the kitchen. Check the water's turned off… Okay. Cold vinyl floor, cupboard doors open, empty shelves, thin film of dust in the sink…

He drew the back-door bolts and stepped out to the yard. The rope on the old wooden clothes pulley had snapped since his last visit and the pulley was hanging askew. He pulled the two ends of the rope together, tied them and hoisted the contraption back into place then stood a moment, eyes closed, picturing a summer Sunday, the sun reflecting off whitewashed walls onto three boys, basking in the heat, engrossed in their books. He opened his eyes and looked at the peeling paint and the dull sky above.

Shivering, he stepped back inside, bolting the door. Moving quickly now he walked through the kitchen with its cold vinyl floor, through the carpeted room with its fifties Devon fireplace to the staircase which rose directly from the room.

Thirteen steps. Steep. Used to go up and down in the dark counting… One… Two…Three… The fourth one creaked if you got the right spot… just…there. He jogged up to the tiny landing, stopped at the little window in the interior wall and glanced through into the front bedroom where his mother and father used to sleep. He looked at…nothing.

He turned left into the empty back bedroom and stopped, eyes closed, seeing the beds which took up almost the whole room space, the only other item a small bedside table. He remembered when he was young lying in the dark, waiting for his brothers to come home, and, later, when they had married, having the room to himself, with space for a wardrobe and a chest of drawers and shelves for his books.

Sighing, he moved to the window and gazed out onto the entry and the rows of back yards, here and there shards of glass and broken bottle bottoms cemented into the tops of the walls to deter thieves. There was grass growing in places between the pieces of glass. Further along Jack Erwin's pigeon shed boasted a new coat of paint.

A movement attracted his attention. A heavily-built man, cigarette dangling from his lips, had appeared at the back door of old Mrs Wilson's house. The man obviously lived there but he didn't know him.

Something snagged the back of his hand and he snatched it back, looking down. The nail head protruded a half-inch or so from the window retaining batten. He remembered leaving it that way the time he replaced the sash cord – just in case it needed adjusting and he had to take the batten off again. He had meant to knock it in but had never got around to it. Apathy rules. He pulled off a shoe and with a couple of hefty swipes drove the nail home.

Replacing his shoe he backed out through the doorway, sucking his hand, and took a long look into both rooms before descending the stairs to the front door.

Well, he thought, that's it, and reached for the door handle.

He hesitated and crossed the room to the fireplace. He stepped onto the hearth and faced the chimney breast, trying to remember. He stroked his fingers across the wallpaper to the seam and then downward to where it met the tiles just to the left of the clock point. Then he carefully picked at the edge of the paper and peeled it back.

There it was – his cartoon of Laurel and Hardy. It was barely visible.

Reaching into his pocket he pulled out a ball pen and slowly inked in the outlines until the little drawing was restored then stepped back, smiling.

The smile faded as he turned and faced the room once more…the papered walls, the patterned carpet and curtains and the built-in glass-doored alcove cabinet where she kept all her china and her family bible where she recorded all the births and marriages and deaths and he closed his eyes once more and he remembered another time when petrol was four bob a gallon, summers never ended and people lived for ever and he remembered the man and the woman and the three boys and he remembered the faces of the man and the woman when he told them about his brother and he turned and went out of the door for the last time slamming it tight and walked away head down against the cold.

FRIENDS IN HIGH PLACES

The first time I saw Herbie McCrea he was standing on a six-inch girder fifty feet above my head, flapping his arms to chase away the cold stiffness of the January morning.

I had just joined the squad, at that time halfway through the erection of the steelwork for an office block on the corner of Piedmont Avenue and the Old Bridgetown Road and one of the fellows was showing me across to the works hut on the far corner of the site. As I buckled on my toolbelt the big yellow-jacketed figure stepped onto the hook of a crane and signalled down to the operator in the cab.

"Who's he?" I asked.

"Who's who?" asked my companion. "Oh… Up there? That's Herbie McCrea. Best steelman in the country. Nowhere he won't go…No nerves." He grinned. "No brains, either."

I watched the crane lower the big man down. When he was still four or five feet from the ground he hopped off and shambled into the hut beside us, coming out a moment later with a monkey wrench.

"Hey, Herbie!" called my companion. The big man turned towards us.

"Meet… What did you say your name was?"

"Donnolly…Jackson Donnolly. But it's only my mother calls me that. Everyone else calls me Jacko."

Herbie gave me a friendly nod and thrust out a hand. I felt my finger joints give a little. "'Call me Shane,'" he said… "Alan Ladd – Shane."

I looked at the other guy but he just chuckled like it was nothing new and walked away.

And that's how it began. We hit it off right from the beginning, Herbie and me. We weren't that far apart age wise and had been steelmen around the same length of time, moving from site to site when the jobs came up. It wasn't an easy life but the money was good, the idea being to make as much as you could as early as you could before the years caught up. And in my case they were beginning to.

Herbie, like I'd been told, wasn't the brightest but he was well liked by everyone. Except Tyrone, that is. First up the ladder in the morning, last down at night, Herbie loved being up there on the girders, ambling along, several storeys high, hands in his pockets like he was out for a Sunday afternoon stroll.

I never found out what it was between him and Artie Tyrone, the squad foreman. From time to time I overheard brief snippets of conversation among the others, but never enough to piece anything together. I never asked any questions for I knew I wouldn't get any answers – I was still a newcomer and steelmen tend to keep their opinions close.

Herbie had a wife who fleeced him of just about everything he earned. I first saw her one payday picking her way across the rubble of the site to a chorus of whistles and whoops from the other guys in the squad. Her reaction was a toss of bleached hair and an exaggerated sway of her hips as she pranced right up to Herbie. She stretched up, plucked his pay packet from his pocket, wiggled her fingers at him, strutted back across the site and out through the gap in the fencing while Herbie just stood there like a big Labrador pup. As she walked away he spoke; "'Of all the gin joints in all the towns in all the world you had to pick this one'…. Humphrey Bogart – Casablanca."

You see, Herbie loved the movies, spending most nights watching old re-runs on television. He knew all the old films by heart, an instant recall on all the scenes, all the dialogue. We'd spend most lunch breaks sitting up there on the beams or in the hut when it rained, listening to his Cary

Grant or Edward G Robinson as he recited all the lines, word and accent perfect, pausing now and then to take a bite of his sandwich.

Oh, yes – his sandwiches. Now, with all the money she took from him you'd think his wife could have put something decent in his sandwiches, right? Peanut butter. Monday to Friday, peanut butter. Weekends even, when we worked them. I mean, you'd expect something special on a Sunday, wouldn't you? But peanut butter was all he ever got.

Once or twice I caught him glancing into my lunchbox. I was lucky that way. My wife always had something different for me – ham, chicken maybe, tuna sometimes.

After a while Herbie took to throwing his sandwiches to the pigeons. I mentioned this to my wife and the next day when I opened my lunchbox there was an extra packet. So what I did was I pretended there was too much for me and gave one to Herbie. You should have seen the way that sandwich disappeared and when I offered him a couple more they went the same way. From that day on I shared my lunch with Herbie and everybody was happy – me, Herbie… the pigeons – for a while, anyhow, until the pigeons got sick of the peanut butter and flew off somewhere else.

The day Herbie saved my life still re-runs in my mind like one of his old movies, the scenes vivid, sharp.

I was up on the sixth level of an apartment block framework at the time, guiding a twenty-foot beam onto a cross girder as the crane lowered it into place. I was holding onto an upright and signalling down to the operator as he inched the beam down. The guy who'd slung it to the hook hadn't done it right for suddenly the beam started to dip and slide through the loops. I tried to get clear and would have been okay but the beam twisted and caught me across the back of the legs. I struggled to keep a grip on the upright and I'm not sure what happened then, it was all so quick, but the next thing I knew I was hanging head down and something was crushing into my leg just behind the knee. I didn't know it at the time, of course, but it seems the chain had snagged round the upright, trapping my leg, leaving me swinging upside down seventy feet above the ground, looking at the inverted parapet of the building opposite, screaming for my life. And then, jerkily, link by link, the chain began to unwind and I felt myself slipping.

They talk about it still. Herbie was up on the next level at the far side of the framework when he heard my screams. They say he came across the girders, arms outstretched like a tightrope walker. By now the chain was rattling free and I could feel it dragging across my leg. I had stopped yelling by this time, gibbering all sorts of promises to the Almighty if He would only give me one more chance.

They tell me Herbie broke into a run along the top of the girder. He grabbed the side upright and slid down it like a fireman down a pole. I heard the pounding of boots above me and at that moment the beam slipped clear of the loops and the chain went slack. The beam clanged against the framework on the way down and I screamed as I began to swing out and away and then, bobbing and spinning, my field of vision changed and a big hand came over the edge of the girder and grabbed me by the belt.

Outside the site fence, a line of white faces stared up as I dangled there in Herbie's firm grip until they came with safety lines and a harness and lowered me to the ground. But I don't remember that bit because I'd passed out long before they got to me.

Herbie's nerve left him around the same time as his wife.

She took off with a Sikh door-to-door salesman two weeks after Christmas. It seems he had been a regular visitor during the day while Herbie was at work. I started to have my suspicions one payday when she arrived at the site wearing a green and yellow sari, holding it high above her knees as she tiptoed round the pools of mud.

Anyway, Herbie got home one night to find she'd gone, leaving a note and a lucky shark's tooth and that's when his world changed. On the following Monday I came across him sitting astride a crossbeam, hugging the upright, his head buried in his sleeve. I touched his shoulder, asked him if he was all right. It was then he told me. I must say it didn't come as a surprise but I didn't tell him that.

"Come on down, Herbie, and we'll have a cup of tea – It'll help to talk about it."

Herbie gripped the upright and shook his head and looked up at me, eyes gone dull. "I can't move, Jacko…I'm scared…I can't move."

Well, naturally, I didn't believe him and tried to coax him to let go of the upright. But I should have known; it wasn't the first time I'd seen that look – Herbie McCrea's days on the steelwork were over.

We got him down in the end. We strapped him into a harness and lowered him, so scared we had to blindfold him, to the ground. When we got there Tyrone was waiting, hands on his fat hips. He took one look at Herbie, threw back his head and started to laugh.

My hand was strapped up for a week afterwards. I waited until he doubled forward, almost choking with merriment, before letting him have it. He staggered back, flopped into a pool of mud and lay there.

By the time he came round Herbie and I were gone.

It wasn't too long after that when Herbie lost it completely. He took to standing by the window, watching the bus stop on the other side of the road, waiting for her to come back. With the arrival of each bus he would crane his neck, checking the dismounting passengers, turning away in despair when she wasn't among them.

By that time my knee was giving trouble and I had to look around for some other work, finishing up on gate security at a hat factory on the outskirts of town, working shifts, hours changing every three weeks. Because of that my visits to Herbie became irregular and as the weeks passed he became increasingly reclusive, rarely leaving the house, hoping, always hoping, she would come back.

I did what I could. I got a spare key to let myself in as he'd stopped answering the doorbell. I made him meals when I could but getting him to eat wasn't easy. By the end of the summer he was down by two stones and refusing to see the doctor in spite of my pleas.

The call came late one night as I was about to climb into bed.

When I got there two police cars were parked at the kerb, an ambulance further back. A group of people, neighbours, huddled together, heads tilted close, whispering, throwing frequent glances. All the lights were out in Herbie's house and both downstairs windows were broken, glass lying on the pavement.

"Been like this the past hour or more." I turned. A policeman had come up behind me. "You Jacko, by any chance?"

I nodded. "What happened?"

The policeman rolled his eyes. "Seems he took some sort of exception to the driver of the number sixteen bus. Started to throw things at him – jars of food. Kept shouting about when was he going to bring her back. Broke two bus windows, scared the hell out of the passengers and the place is covered in peanut butter if the labels are anything to go by. It's like a skating rink out there. We could force our way in but they say he's a big fellow and we don't want anybody to get hurt if we can help it." He hesitated. "He says he won't talk to anybody but you. You want to try?... It's not that you have to, but he's bolted the door and we'd have to break it down and we want to avoid that. The neighbours speak well of him and that's another reason... We don't wish him any harm."

"Ok," I said. "I'll talk to him."

I went over to the window and peered in. I thought I saw movement over towards the fireplace. Wary of the broken glass I leaned forward.
" Herbie," I called. "It's me."

I heard a rustling noise. "Jacko?...That you, Jacko?"

"Let me in, Herbie. Unbolt the door and let me in."

"The bolt's out...I took it out a while ago."

I turned round. The policeman was over at one of the cars. Trying to appear casual, I went to the door, quickly put in my key and twisted. The door opened and I looked over my shoulder at the policeman. He started to move forward, slipped and fell against the bonnet of the car. He straightened, checked the sole of his boot, grimaced and scraped it on the kerb edge. I stepped inside and closed the door again.

I felt my way along the narrow hall to the living room and looked round the door frame. I fumbled for the light switch and snapped it on, squinting in the sudden glare.

Herbie was sitting cross-legged in his underpants in the middle of the floor. He was plucking at an Indian rug in front of him. There were wisps of wool everywhere – on the floor, the table, the chairs – wisps of wool that stirred and curled in the draught from the hole in the window.

He didn't look up. He was hunched over, concentrating on the rug, humming softly in tune to the music from the room above. *As Time Goes By.* Then, all of a sudden, he shivered, dropped his head to his chest and began to sob.

I knelt beside him with some difficulty and put my hand on his shoulder. I said it was okay, it was okay. He mumbled something but I couldn't make it out.

"What was that, Herbie? What did you say?"

He spoke again. He said; "'Frankly, my dear, I don't give a damn'... Clarke Gable – Gone With The Wind."

They took him away. He offered no resistance and by the time they'd stopped sticking needles into him he didn't know Rambo from Old Mother Riley. They allowed me to ride with him in the ambulance as he lay strapped into the narrow cot, drifting in and out of sleep, all the way to the hospital.

Less than twenty-four hours later he was in another ambulance on his way to Greenacre Institute for the psychologically disturbed.

"You're mad," I said, immediately regretting my choice of words.

Herbie spread his big hands on the formica table top. "I know – that's why I'm here."

"Aw, Herbie," I mumbled. "You know I didn't mean it like that."

He nodded, face turning towards the barred window.

Feeling guilty, I looked around the room. There were a dozen or so others – some patients, some visitors. The place didn't change much, the walls still the pale washed-out blue they'd been since I'd been coming to see Herbie, almost six years now. The scrubbed vinyl floor covering had patches here and there, the tables strategically arranged to hide them as much as possible.

Herbie looked in good shape. He'd put on a few pounds, yet every time I saw him he looked sadder than the time before.

He turned towards me again. I shook my head and watched a nurse lead an old man in a dressing gown out of the room. "I can't, Herbie. It just wouldn't work – something would go wrong and we'd both be in trouble. Anyway, you're due to get out soon. What's the big hurry?"

Herbie dropped his head but not before I caught the guilty look.

"You are getting out soon, aren't you?… Herbie?"

Herbie swallowed, big hands starting to fidget with his mug.

"Actually…"

"Actually what?… Exactly actually what?"

Herbie was looking everywhere…everywhere but at me. "Something happened yesterday…I don't know now when I'm going to get out."

I stared at him. He was looking over my shoulder now, his expression changing.

I turned. A heavy-set nurse, greasy black hair, tattooed forearms walked past. He glowered at Herbie. At least he tried to. It wasn't easy with his left eye and all.

I sighed. "Aw, Herbie."

"Well, he asked for it, Jacko. He was shoving Norman about…teasing him." His eyes followed the nurse. "'Go ahead, punk…make my day'… Clint Eastwood – Dirty Harry."

The male nurse went over to the window, reached between the bars and closed the catch. He turned towards Herbie, slowly patted the bars, smiled and walked out of the room.

Herbie watched him throughout. "So now you know, Jacko. They're not going to let me out – not for a long time, anyhow. That's why you've got to help me. I'm okay again and I know I can do it."

"Herbie, we're not young men anymore. Anyway, my knee couldn't take it."

"Then I'll do it on my own, Jacko. All you have to do is find one and be waiting for me outside the wall. I know a way to get out, but we're miles from anywhere and I need to get away quickly or they'll catch me. I need your help…Will you do it, Jacko?"

I hesitated. Then; "I'm sorry, Herbie." I couldn't look him in the eye.

There was a long silence before he spoke again; "I thought you were my friend." He scraped back his chair. Stood. Turned away.

…and at that moment the beam slipped clear of the loops and the chain went slack. The beam clanged against the framework on the way down and I screamed as I began to swing out and away and then, bobbing and spinning, my field of vision changed and a big hand came over the edge of the girder and grabbed me by the belt……

"Wait," I said.

I stood in the shadow of the high stone wall. He was late. One o'clock, he'd said and it was almost twenty past. Somewhere far off a dog started to bark. Another joined in.

A set of headlights approached the bend. I ducked behind a bush and when the car passed, straightened, rubbed my knee.

I checked my watch again. The moon disappeared behind a cloud, the dogs still howling, and I hunched into my jacket.

"'Listen to them…children of the night.'" The voice in my ear made me jump. "Bela Lugosi – Dracula." Herbie stood there, unbuttoning a white coat, a couple of sizes too small. He shoved it under a bush. "Where's the car?"

"Perfect!...Perfect!" Herbie hopped up and down like a kid, rubbing his hands. He looked up at the top of the crane, nearly two hundred feet above, the jib pointing off towards the city centre, a mile or so away. The faint breeze ruffled his hair. The sky was patchy with cloud, the moon casting a faint glow over the site. "Let's go, Jacko. Let's go."

I slung the satchel over my shoulder and followed him uneasily across to the perimeter fence. Herbie gripped the top links, pulled himself up, swung his legs over and dropped to the other side. I hesitated, shook my head, and did the same but not without difficulty. My knee was acting up. It had got a lot worse in recent times and arthritis was well settled in. Give it a couple of years and I would need a stick.

I limped after Herbie, surprised how easy it had been to get into the site. If two middle-aged guys could do it so could a kid. I determined to phone the contractors in the morning – anonymously, of course.

Herbie was waiting at the foot of the crane. "Okay, Jacko?…Okay?" He reached for the ladder rising up the inside of the tower and started to climb. I let him get up twenty feet or so then stepped onto the bottom rung.

I was slow. It had been over seven years since I last made a climb like that and I was out of condition. Each time I put my weight on my bad knee the pain stabbed into me. Herbie, however, was climbing above me like a monkey and already forty feet up.

"Herbie!" I hissed. "For God's sake slow down!" But I'd have been better saving my breath for the climb.

It wasn't long, though, in spite of the throbbing in my knee, before I started to get a feeling of exhilaration. I glanced down at the trenches and building materials below. And that's when the adrenalin started to flow and the old almost forgotten thrill came sweeping back. I realised I was smiling.

I was still smiling when my head bumped into something hard. It was Herbie's boot. I looked up. "What's the matter?"

"I need to go," shouted Herbie.

"Go? Go where?"

"You know – Go!" I heard the sound of a zip.

"Herbie! We're a hundred feet in the air, for God's sake – Why didn't you go before we started?"

"Sorry, Jacko…I can't help it – It's just I can't hold on like I used to."

I groaned, wrapped my arms round the ladder, tucked in my head, closed my eyes and prayed there'd be no sudden change in the direction of the wind. I waited.

"Ok, you can look up again." Herbie recommenced climbing.

It was harder now and we were both getting slower. I could hear Herbie puffing over the sound of my own laboured breathing and I was taking most of the strain on my arms to save my knee. The steel legs of the crane glinted in the moonlight and I paused to shift the satchel into a more comfortable position.

I reckon we were about thirty feet from the underside of the cabin when Herbie stopped again. I was glad of the break, but when after a minute there was no sign of him moving, I called up. "It's okay, Herbie, I'm all right. On you go."

But he still didn't move.

"What is it this time? You can't need to pee again."

There was no response. I pulled myself up until I could tug his trouser leg. "Come on, Herbie. The sooner we get this whole thing out of your system, the sooner I can be home in bed…Herbie?"

I got it then. I couldn't see his face but I didn't need to. His arms were wrapped round the ladder and he was shaking. Only this time there were no workmates, no safety harness to get him down.

He said the two words I didn't want him to say; "I'm afraid."

So that's the way it was; two hundred feet up a tower crane, in the middle of the night, and nobody about. I couldn't leave him while I climbed down and went for help and I couldn't hold out much longer myself if we stayed where we were.

I shouted at him again but got no reaction. I looked round in desperation, trying to think. Then I remembered the other time, all those years ago. It probably wouldn't work, but…

"Did you see him down there, Herbie? He's laughing…Tyrone…Do you hear him?...Listen…Can you hear him?" A soft wind sighed round the tower.

Herbie jerked. "What?...Tyrone?...Down there?...Where are you, Tyrone? I'll show you!…I'll show you!... 'Fill your hands, you sonofabitch!'…John Wayne! – True Grit!" And then he was climbing, hand over hand, almost jumping from rung to rung. He reached the underside of the cabin, stretched sideways and swung out from the ladder, clambering up the outside of the cabin. He threw a leg over the bottom rail and stood up on the narrow catwalk running out along the length of the jib.

Fighting for breath I dragged myself up the last few rungs and pushed open the trapdoor of the cabin, crawled inside and limped over to the windscreen.

Herbie was standing upright on the jib. He was yelling; "Look at me, Tyrone! Look at me now!"

I opened the windscreen and leaned out, scared of what I'd done. "Herbie! For God's sake, calm down!... Calm down!" But he was moving away from me out along the catwalk, shuffling sideways, holding onto the rail.

I hinged the roof hatch back and climbed out onto the platform. A cloud shut out the moonlight for a moment and Herbie disappeared from sight. I grasped the top rail and hauled myself onto the catwalk. "Come back, Herbie! That's far enough!" But as the moon reappeared there he was, more than halfway out along the jib, the wind gusting through his hair.

Then he did the craziest thing.

He heaved himself up throwing one leg over the top rail and sat up, straddling it, facing away from me.

I knew. "No, Herbie!...Don't!"

He was thirty feet out. He pushed himself onto his knees and slowly stood up, waving his arms for balance. I closed my eyes. Then I heard him laugh, low at first, getting louder. I opened my eyes. He was standing on the top rail, arms spread wide. He threw back his head. "'Made it, Ma!... Top of the world!'...James Cagney! – White Heat!"

I got down on all fours and began to crawl out towards him. It took me a long time and when I was just beneath him I pulled myself up, holding on tightly to the side. "Herbie...Please come down...Please?"

He was standing absolutely still on the rail. Then he looked down at me like he was seeing me for the first time. "That you, Jacko?...That you?"

Something caught in my throat. "Yes...It's me...It would be a good idea if you came down now, Herbie, don't you think?" I spoke like I was speaking to a child.

He stood on a moment, looked round him, shrugged and reached down a big hand. I took it, guided him down onto the catwalk and he grabbed me and we swayed there, hanging onto each other.

Then he started to laugh again.

We sat side by side out at the end of the jib watching the city skyline, legs dangling in space. I thought I heard a siren somewhere.

I rummaged in the satchel and pulled out two cans of beer. I handed one over and dug into the satchel again. "Sandwich?" His eyes widened. "Roast beef," I said.

"Aw, Jacko... Just like the old days, eh? "

I nodded. "Yes..." A set of headlights was approaching and the noise of the siren faded. Then another set of lights, slowing down. "... Just like the old days."

Herbie took a bite, a sip from the can. He sighed in contentment.

I leaned forward and looked down. The lights had stopped directly below us and I heard a door slam. Then another. "'Who are those guys?'" I said.

Herbie looked at me. "Huh?"

"'Who are those guys?'... Paul Newman – Butch Cassidy And The Sundance Kid."

Herbie was still looking at me. The breeze ruffled his hair. "Butch who?" he asked.

I started to laugh. Herbie was still looking blankly at me. I put my hand on his shoulder. "Never mind...Drink your beer."

He hadn't seen them. He would soon enough and I didn't want to ruin the little time left. I listened to him slurp his beer as we sat there high above the rooftops, the first faint glimmer of day rising over the river like curtain lights, the black silhouettes of the high rises changing to grey-gold, the end of the reel, the screen turning to blank.

THE BACK OF MY BROTHER'S HEAD

When we were young, my brother and I, we shared the back bedroom of our parents' little two up, two down until he turned eighteen and went off to university in Scotland. We had this old walnut dresser with scratched panels and a loose handle. It had three mirrors, one in the centre which tilted back and one either side which swivelled inwards so that if you leaned forward far enough and got the angles right you could see the back of your own head. I could comb my hair taking all the time I needed to shape it into a perfect D.A. to match the Tony Curtis bob at the front.

The last thing I want to see these days is the back of my head, the Tony Curtis long gone – like most of my hair and the thirty-inch waistline.

My brother now. He still has all his hair and he's had it trimmed in the past few days so it's looking good – from the back anyway. I haven't seen the front yet nor have I seen his face…

He's two rows – two pews – in front of me. Beside him is his wife. Naomi and I don't hit it off too well. Not, I should say, that we're openly antagonistic to one another. It's just I've always sensed this air of superiority waft in my direction when we're together in the same room. Still, I've got to say she's looking good, too, and, besides, she and Mary always got on well.

"It's your imagination, Andy," she used to say to me, Mary did. "She's always been a good friend to me." And so Naomi was, I got to admit that.

In front of my brother stands his daughter, Emma... and Toby, her-about-to-be- any-minute-now husband.

Toby is an asshole. How it got this far I'll never understand. I've seen the bruises on Emma's arms and one of those rare nights I called – rare because of the Naomi thing – the side of her face was swollen and she'd been crying. Why in God's name my brother and Naomi gave their consent I'll never know. Me? I'd have sorted it – and Toby – out a long time ago if it had been anything to do with me.

Which it doesn't.

I have two sons. They're sitting either side of me. Barry has his wife, carrying my first grandchild, on his far side and Dave has this month's girlfriend beside him.

We see a lot of each other, Barry, Dave and me, working together the way we do. We're getting by at the moment but the building trade's not doing too well. We've enough to keep us going another six months or so. But after that......

It's done. The minister has pronounced them man and wife and told the groom he may kiss the bride, which he does. Then after he's said a few more words they all traipse out of the church towards the room at the back to sign the register – the bride, the groom, the bridesmaid and best man, Toby's parents, Naomi...my brother. As he steps out of the pew and stands aside to let Naomi past I get to see his face. He looks like he's okay. But I'm his brother and I know......

When Mary and I got married the photographer came, set up his tripod, a few quick clicks and he was away in half an hour. I have one of the photographs, just the two of us, framed now and sitting beside my bed. It's black and white, of course, but each time when I wake up and look at it I see something different.

We've been hanging around the hotel lobby since half past one, waiting for the photographer to finish. It's now almost half three and my stomach thinks it's had a by-pass. It's a cold April day and I've had three Guinness and three Jamesons and I need to eat soon or I'll...

That's my problem. Used to be I could take it or leave it but since last autumn I've found it difficult. Barry and Dave keep an eye on me and I do try. I do. Really, I try......

The meal's over and the speeches, too, thank God.

My brother's was very short. He started off with the joke about the similarity between a good speech and a mini skirt, you know the one. It raised a few polite laughs and an uncontrolled outburst from an uncle of Toby's who must have come in from the Outer Hebrides or somewhere. When he got to the bit about welcoming Toby into the family I looked away.

Next was the best man, weedy little git. You think my brother's was bad? At least he had an excuse but this guy was as funny as a colonoscopy. He went on for about ten minutes then took a coughing fit and had to be thumped on the back by the wife of the guy with the laugh.

Toby's speech? Sorry. Missed it. Went for a pee.

Emma.

Emma looks a dream. She's twenty-two and the daughter I never had. When she was a kid she used to come everywhere with us – Mary, the boys, Emma, me.

We went camping a lot then. I taught her to fish. We would sit there on the riverbank, the four of us, Mary off somewhere with her sketchpad, and I'd show her how to bait, cast, reel in…..

If she was the daughter Mary and I never had, she was a sister to Barry and Dave. School holidays would find her staying with us – picking up bad habits no doubt, Naomi would say to my brother. Not only did she learn to fish she could plane a straight edge or cut out a dovetail joint good as my sons. When Barry broke up with his first girl she sat at the kitchen table getting him through his first black night.

She's down at the far end of the room, talking to my brother. I watch his face. He's still trying hard but he can't hide it from me…..

The Eagles are telling us to take it easy. Boy, but it's hot in here. I loosen my tie. The chairs and tables have all been pushed out to the walls and the floor is vibrating with dancers – all ages, all shapes, all sizes. I push myself up and hold onto the table a moment till everything steadies. Then I walk towards the French windows for some air. A tall blonde in a blue dress sways in front of me and I do a quick shuffle round her. She laughs and claps my shoulder.

Naomi is standing in front of me. I wiggle my fingers and gyrate my hips. She looks at me with disapproval. "Andrew…Are you drunk?"

"Drunk? – Me?" I say. "Do birds crap in the trees?"

She gives me a look of disgust and marches off in the direction of the ladies, handbag under her arm.

I look about for my sons. Barry is dancing with Emma, eyes skimming the room, Dave over at the bar, talking to a guy in a cream suit, pink tie. I'll remind him about it on the site in the morning.

The music stops and the DJ comes in with his patter. Then I see Toby making his way in the direction of the alcove leading to the gents. He goes in. I look across at Dave and he says something to the guy in the cream suit and grins and walks towards the alcove, Barry already off the dance floor heading in the same direction.

I wait. From where I stand I have a clear view. Barry pushes open the door and goes in. Dave stands outside, back to the door.

The DJ is urging everyone back onto the dance floor and the music has started again. The dancers have their hands on their hips, twisting their bodies, bending forward. *The Timewarp.*

The best man walks into the alcove and Dave gives him a broad smile and starts to chat. Dave is a motormouth – talk to anyone, anytime, anywhere about anything. The best man seems anxious to get past but Dave, still talking, still smiling puts his hand on his arm and I see his knuckles whiten. The best man looks round as if seeking help then backs away and walks towards the lobby to look for another toilet.

After a minute the door of the gents opens and Barry comes out, straightens his tie, says something to Dave, looks across at me and nods. I nod back. Then they both walk over to the bar.

It isn't long. The door opens again and Toby comes out. He looks like he's just received a lunch invitation from Hannibal Lecter. His collar is sticking up and the lapels of his wedding suit are crumpled. Then his cheeks bulge and he turns and rushes back into the gents.

I sense someone beside me. I look round and Naomi is there. She has seen the whole thing. She looks at me for what seems a long time then turns and goes over to my brother and sits down beside him.

It's nearly midnight. I'm knackered. I've been up since daybreak and we need to be on the site before eight tomorrow morning to sign for a delivery of roof trusses.

The music is different now, quieter. A girl is singing. She sounds like she's in the room with us. Her voice is clear and achingly beautiful and I've heard the song before but never like this. The dancers are moving slow, circling on the same spot. The lights are dim and I don't want the song to end.

"You miss her, don't you?"

I look up. Naomi is standing beside me. I don't know how long she's been there. I pull out a chair and she sits down. She, too, is tired. It is there in the set of her eyes.

The girl sings about the passing of the years… summer days… fields of gold…..

Mary.

Dark grey eyes. Long hair, black as a raven's wing. Summer, 1969. Somehow she had got the rear wheel of her car stuck in the track gouged out by a digger. "Please can you help me?" she asked, her face flushed with the embarrassment of her predicament. She worked for an architect, there to hand over a set of plans to the builder. We got together, a few of us, and with planks and a bit of manpower freed the car and she was soon on her way. In less than a minute I'd got her work phone number from the plans…..

A soft guitar melody now and the girl begins another verse… sad… haunting…..

Mary. Black hair, faint streaks of silver, urchin cut now, humming with contentment, sketching her landscapes of green and yellow and gold as we watched the seasons come and leave. Mary, the look on her face when they told her the results of the tests and in too, too short a time the hair almost pure silver and the skin of her face stretched and pallid, the eyes retaining that gleam of burnished pewter. "He's not for her," she'd whispered when she heard about the engagement. "He's not for her."

Summer days… I look down at the table. It's scattered with glasses and napkins and place cards and, here and there, the petals of flowers. "Yes," I say.

"She was my best friend," says Naomi. I nod. It's been the longest of winters. I reach for my glass but I don't pick it up. Naomi stretches forward, puts her hand on top of mine for a moment, squeezes. "Thank you," she says. She rises from the chair and walks back across the room to my brother.

The girl has stopped singing, the melody fades and there is no sound, no passage of time…

Then all the chairs around me scrape back and Barry and his wife and Dave and his girl sit down around me. Nobody speaks and then the DJ says, "That was the late, great…" And I never get to hear the singer's name because Dave starts to talk.

It's an early start tomorrow and we walk towards the door. Emma is there in the lobby along with my brother and Naomi. Toby is nowhere to be seen. Emma comes to me and I open my arms and she hugs me and I wish her every happiness and let her go as she turns to my sons and their women. I look at Naomi and, I'm not kidding about this, she walks over to me, stands on tiptoes, kisses me on the cheek. I feel the warmth.

My brother.

My brother and I have hardly spoken all day. Which isn't all that unusual. The older we get the harder we find it to communicate. Not that it matters anymore in this extra-sensory life we've come to share. He knows and I know. Like, for instance, he doesn't need to tell me how unhappy he is. And I don't need to tell him that I'd do anything to make it right for him.

He takes my hand and I hold it tight. "Thanks for a great day," I manage to say and he summons up a smile for he doesn't want me to worry about him.

The taxi motor is running and he lets go my hand and turns back in towards the reception room, Naomi on one side, Emma on the other.

The air is sharp and clean and I stand on the steps and suck in a deep breath and turn and look back.

People are crowding about, some getting ready to leave, waving their goodbyes, some, believe it or not, just arriving, shouting their greetings. Some carry wine glasses, one woman carries her shoes, padding about in her stocking feet and I stretch to full height, looking past the mass of bodies milling back and forth, searching, squinting in the bright light of the lobby, trying to catch a glimpse of the back of my brother's head.

CHILDREN'S HOUR

Belfast, 1997

Out in the open air, much to his relief, his ears popped clear and the dull underwater-like sounds of the flight were replaced by the sharp whine of engines and the swish of traffic on the dual carriageway beyond the terminal perimeter fence.

He walked across to the line of taxis and one of the men broke away from the group sheltering under the overhang of the roof and approached him, reaching out to take the worn canvas overnight bag, placing it in the boot and opening the taxi's rear door.

"Where to, sir?" the man asked as he lowered himself onto the seat, the strong smell of air-freshener, the sign on the back of the driver's headrest thanking him for not smoking.

Raymond didn't answer right away. Throughout the flight he'd been thinking about this, tempted to book in somewhere if that somewhere was cheap enough. He'd even wondered, since Dee had phoned, if he should come over at all. The driver was eyeing him in the rear-view mirror, waiting for a response. Raymond leaned forward and gave him the address.

The rainwater lay in pools on the tarmac. The wheels of the taxi thrummed quietly towards the exit and out onto the dual carriageway.

They would have to go left as far as the roundabout before circling back towards the city and on to the northern suburbs and the old house where, until yesterday, his father had lived since Raymond was a child.

He gazed out at the passing cityscape and pictured the house, practically derelict and bought for a song, the painstaking restoration by his father – stripping staircase spindles, replacing plaster corbels, renewing moulded skirting, while Roddy and he lay on the rug in front of the fire, listening to the radio. Often they'd be joined by Dee, six months younger than Raymond, just as it turned five o'clock when they'd be welcomed to another Children's Hour and the adventures of Norman and Henry Bones, Boy Detectives, or Sheila St Clair with her Family Zoo and a fox called Miranda.

The taxi was crossing the new bridge now, over to his right the all-glass Royal Mail building reflecting the dull October sky. He wondered should he have put on his tie, but his bag was in the boot and anyway the tie was all bright greens and blues, hardly appropriate at this time.

They left the motorway at Fortwilliam and in a matter of minutes turned into the short cul-de-sac. "Which number, sir?" asked the driver and Raymond pointed the house out. There were cars parked on both sides. The driver stopped in the middle of the road and retrieved the canvas bag from the boot. Raymond paid him and looked across at the old house, a little surprised at its condition – not shabby exactly, but heading that way. Okay, his father had been getting on a bit but Roddy was still there, right?

Shabby. Raymond glanced down at his suit. His trousers were badly in need of pressing, his shoes had seen better days. He'd been meaning to buy a new suit for some time now but, moneywise, he never seemed to be able to get ahead, a big chunk of what he made going on the boys' maintenance. What with the air fare and everything he reckoned he'd have to start all over again.

He walked over to the gate. It wouldn't give at first but eventually jerked open. It had swollen with the rain and when he tried to close it behind him it clunked against the gatepost and swung open again. He left it that way, walked up the path and rang the doorbell.

He heard footsteps in the hallway and the door opened and Dee stood there.

She didn't say anything but leaned into him and held him close. He put his arms round her and they stood like that for a moment before she broke away, still holding his arm. "I'm sorry, Ray…I'm so sorry."

He nodded; "Thanks for letting me know." He followed her into the hall.

"He…Your dad's in the front room…I'll make some tea. Roddy had to go into town to sort out some arrangements. There's no one else here at the moment but people have been in and out all day…" She opened the door of the front room and stepped back. "You'll want a minute by yourself."

Death has a smell of its own, a cloying mixture of flowers and decay that stays with you until the last mourner has gone, leaving you nothing but the letters and the old photographs and the sudden trigger of memory. He walked across to his father.

There is a belief that death transmogrifies, making the dead look young again but all Raymond could see was every year of the old man's life sealed into the lines of his face. The room was silent save for the slow tick of the clock on the mantelpiece. Raymond looked down at his father and……

……Early spring and the blossom on the cherry tree in the corner of the garden. They had been with their mother in town and on arriving home she couldn't find her key. She had asked Raymond, the older by two years, to run down to the shop and get his father's key.

It was coming up on five o'clock and Raymond covered the half mile in record time, anxious to get back before the start of what was to be the last ever broadcast of Children's Hour after over forty years on air.

When he entered the shop his father, normally behind the hardware counter, was nowhere to be seen. Presuming him to be in the rear storeroom, and deciding to spring a surprise, Raymond tiptoed round the counter. He put his ear to the door, listened to the muffled sounds, pushed open the door and ran into the room.

The woman jumped back, his father turning quickly from her, the woman's cry of embarrassment, the look of guilt on his father's face now one of anguish.

Raymond, nine years old, stood there, not quite sure what to make of it all but knowing that in that instant everything had changed. He started to back out of the storeroom.

His father spoke; "Raymond!... Wait a minute!... Wait out in the shop!... I need to speak to you... Wait...Son?... Please?"

Raymond went into the shop and stood beside the stock of screws and nails and bolts, graded for length and gauge. He plunged his hand into the tub of galvanised roofing nails, squeezing, squeezing till the blood started to seep out between his fingers.

He heard his father come up behind him but he didn't look round. "It's not what you think," his father whispered. "It's not..." He stopped.

Raymond let go of the nails, blood dripping into the tub.

"You've cut yourself." His father reached over his shoulder and wrapped his handkerchief round his hand. "Hold that tight – It'll stop the bleeding."

The woman came out of the store and walked quickly past them. Raymond recognised her now as a frequent customer when he helped out during school holidays. Head turned away from him she opened the door and went out.

"You won't tell your mother, now...Sure you won't?"

Raymond shook his head. "Mum sent me to get your door key – she can't find hers." His father reached into his pocket and held out his key. Their hands touched and Raymond felt the roughness of the skin, the calluses. He went out of the shop without looking back.

Later, listening to Children's Hour for the last time he began to cry and Roddy and Dee looked on as his mother took him in her arms. "Never mind," she said, holding him close. "There'll be other programmes just as good. You wait and see."......

"He asked about you...just before he died...He asked about you."

Raymond turned. Roddy was standing in the doorway. He wore a dark suit, pale blue shirt, black tie. A little older, hair a little thinner. Again Raymond became conscious of his own appearance. He didn't know what to say to his brother. Not for the first time he tried to work out the moment when the gap had opened up, widened. On the rare occasion when they had been together, just the two of them, he had been on the point of raising the matter but, fearful of what he might hear, had taken the easy option, hoping Roddy would say something first. But Roddy never had.

When Roddy and Dee had married, Roddy had asked Dee's brother to be best man. Raymond could still hear his father's words; "Talk about stuck-up," he'd said. "Can't even ask his own brother to stand for him." It wasn't long after that when Raymond, little reason now to stay, had packed a single suitcase and caught the night ferry for Liverpool.

The last time he'd been back was when his mother had died – God, is it four years already? He had thought; Well, here's the chance – surely now he'll talk to me, tell me what this is all about and then maybe we can be the way we used to be all those years ago when we played at boy detectives. Out of nowhere came the thought: which one was the older? Was it Norman or Henry?

"You look well, Roddy," he said.

His brother took a long time to reply; "You, too."

"I've made some tea," Dee called from the kitchen and at the same time the doorbell rang.

"I'll get it," said Roddy and turned away. Raymond went towards the kitchen, in no mood to talk to any of the callers. He'd see them soon enough.

"Is there a plain one I could borrow?" Raymond looked at the green and blue tie.

Dee set the dish on the draining board. "I'll get you one." She was gone a couple of minutes, reappearing, holding out a black tie. "This was your dad's." He took it, knotted it in place. Dee reached up and straightened the knot.

"Which one was the older?" asked Raymond.

"What?"

"Sorry – I was thinking out loud…Norman and Henry Bones…You remember them – the boy detectives…Children's Hour?...Who was the older? Was it Norman or Henry?"

"I remember…I don't know…Norman, maybe?"

Raymond chuckled. "We never missed it when we were kids."

"A million years ago."

"Longer." She only came up to his shoulder. He reached out and touched her cheek. "You never changed, Dee…Not like the rest of us." Her eyes were closed. He took his hand away, stepped back from her. "Time I faced the rest of the clan." He reached for the door handle.

"Ray?"

He looked back. Her hands were tightly clasped in front of her. "Norman – I think it was Norman."

"Yes…me too." He opened the door. "Definitely Norman."

Sometime towards ten o'clock Raymond wandered through the kitchen and out to the back of the house. The workshop door was locked and he backtracked to the kitchen and searched through the keys on the hook, selecting a couple of likely ones. He went out again and at the second try the lock clicked open and he pushed open the door.

He felt along the wall, switched on the light. The tools hung on racks all about him – chisels and saws and planes for woodworking, an electric drill on a horizontal stand, a mitre for cutting joints. A lathe took up almost half of one side of the workshop and down at the far end hung racks of drill bits separated for wood, metal, brick. A bench grinder was bolted to a stand and he flicked the switch. It started up with a whine, gaining speed, settling down to a quiet hum. He switched off the power and it freewheeled to a stop.

All about was the smell of light oil. He picked up an old jack plane, felt the edge of the blade. It was well worn to one side from constant use but still sharp. Searching around, he found a container of wood preservative and poured some into an empty tin, picked up a paintbrush and the jack plane and walked out along the side of the house.

He pushed the gate towards the closed position and knelt, running his hand down to the spot where it met the post. A splinter of wood pierced his palm and he jerked his hand back. He tried to suck out the splinter but it was in too deep. Working by the light of the street lamp he ran the plane down the edge of the gate, the slivers of wood curling and falling to the ground. He tried the gate again and it swung cleanly, the latch clicking into place. He released it, dabbed the preservative onto the bare wood, closed the gate and carried everything back to the workshop.

It was raining again.

He stood, back to the room, gazing out of the window at the overgrown back lawn that stretched down to the rear wall beyond which lay the walkway and the fringe of parkland.

The service had been brief. Roddy had stood opposite Raymond, hands clasped, head lowered. Beside him Uncle Henry, on the hip replacement waiting list, shifted painfully on the uneven grassy slope.

"Ashes to ashes…" The handfuls of clay thudded in synchrony to the intonations of the minister and then the mourners were forming up to shake his hand, word clumsy, anxious to get off the hill and away from the cold north-easterly, scudding across the graveyard with the rain on its tail.

Now, as Raymond looked out on the fine drizzle, settling web-like on the grass, Uncle Henry and a neighbour of his father were debating the merits of Wilkinson over Spear and Jackson and a clink of dishes came from the kitchen as the women finished the washing-up.

His father's sister, Aunt Elsie, was twittering as Roddy helped her into her coat; "We really must try to keep in touch more, dear, we only see each other at funerals. It isn't right, you know, and you're really so fortunate to have someone as wonderful as Deirdre." And her face starting to quiver and embracing Roddy and Roddy, hesitant, putting his hand lightly on her back and staring over her shoulder at the wall.

Taking their cue, the others prepared to leave, all, Raymond noticed, smelling slightly of wood preservative, the men awkwardly shaking hands, the dry kisses of the women, the sudden quiet, and as the last car door slammed and the last engine revved and faded away, Roddy turned and left the room.

Dee came over and stood beside Raymond. "Do you have to go back tonight?" No need now to pretend otherwise she looked tired, her eyes dull.

He thought about it. Perhaps he could, even at this stage, get his flight changed. She obviously wanted him to stay and he would have liked to spend a little longer with her – he didn't know when he'd be back again… if at all.

He heard a crash followed by a splintering sound and a heavy thud and the clatter of metal on metal. He went to the window. His father's toolbox lay on its side, contents spilling onto the gravel. The workshop door was open and as he watched a saw clattered against the toolbox and bounced up the path.

Raymond ran out of the room, through the kitchen and out into the rain, heavier now, blowing round the corner of the house. There were other tools lying on the ground – chisels, screwdrivers, a set of spanners, the jack plane.

Roddy came out of the workshop, arms filled with tools. He dropped them beside the others and went back in.

"Oh, God! – What's he doing? Stop him!" Dee was behind Raymond, a look, a mixture of bewilderment and horror, on her face.

A loud banging came from inside the workshop. Raymond went to the doorway. Roddy had a sledgehammer in his hands and he swung it at the lathe. There were sparks as the hammer hit the end of the lathe and bounced out of his grip. He snatched up a crowbar and prised at the lathe where it was bolted to the bench. He shouted in frustration and hurled the crowbar at the window, smashing the glass out onto the flowerbed.

Dee was screaming now, hands at her face; "Stop it! For God's sake, stop it!"

Roddy lifted the sledgehammer again and pounded at the racks of tins tools, splintering handles, bending blades.

Raymond grabbed his brother round the waist and Roddy shook him off, Raymond stumbling backwards out into the rain, Roddy following, hammer raised.

They stood there, facing one another, both breathing heavily.

"What was the secret?" shouted Roddy.

"What? – What are you talking about?"

"Come on, Raymond! You know what I mean! They were his last words – 'Raymond kept the secret'! I always knew there was something between you two because he didn't give a damn about me! All my life it was Raymond this, Raymond that!" Roddy was gulping air now. "When I was fourteen I was in the school play, remember? No, of course you wouldn't remember. Well, he promised to come and see me. For weeks beforehand he kept promising. When the night came round he didn't show up. Why? Because he took you to a football match! That's the way it always was. He showed no interest in me. And in spite of all that I was the one who stayed to look after him. You…you cleared off and I stayed and still all I ever got was; 'Raymond used to…' or 'That's not the way Raymond would do it'…Well, he's dead now and you know what? – I don't feel a thing!" He was still holding the hammer. He let it drop and stood there, head raised, the rain washing away the tears.

Raymond reached out to touch his brother but Roddy moved back then stepped around him and walked towards the house. "Mind you don't miss your flight." He slammed the door behind him.

Raymond turned to Dee. She stood, trance-like, hair plastered over her forehead, clothes soaking in the rain. He looked at the tools scattered around him, the shards of glass in the flowerbed.

"The bleeding never stops," he said.

He sat in the departure lounge, nursing a plastic cup of coffee. Every now and then an announcement came over the system. There were a few other people in the lounge, among them a young couple over near the far corner, a baby in the girl's lap. They looked little more than teenagers. The baby was asleep and the young man pushed his forefinger into the child's tiny clasp as if to convince himself it was real. The girl spoke and the young man smiled at her.

The door opened behind Raymond and a woman in an overall passed him hawking a vacuum cleaner. He felt a slight chill and pulled his jacket more tightly round him.

The woman plugged the cleaner into a wall socket, switched it on and began to cover the carpet with long methodical sweeps. A hostess with a clipboard stood chatting to a security guard over by the check-in.

"Will passengers for Jersey European flight number JY745 to Leeds-Bradford please proceed to the departure gate…Passengers for Jersey European flight number JY745 to Leeds-Bradford, please proceed to the departure gate."

The young couple with the baby gathered their hand luggage and walked away in the direction of the lounge exit. The woman finished sweeping the carpet and unplugged the vacuum cleaner. She straightened up, hand going to the small of her back.

The departure lounge was quiet. Raymond looked at the clock. He had over an hour yet. His coffee had gone cold and his suit was damp and his hand throbbed where the wood splinter was still embedded, the surrounding skin red and swollen. He felt tired. He tried to make himself a little more comfortable, hunching down into the seat, closing his eyes… and in a while, in that moment between consciousness and sleep, he thought he heard those long-ago words – reassuring, full of comfort, as they always had been before the beginning of this other life; "Goodnight, children – everywhere."

CHICKEN

Belfast, October 1962

My foot slipped on the wet surface of the platform and I went down on one knee, almost losing my grip on the bar. I felt the sharp tug on my jacket as Gusty dragged me towards him, both of us off balance now, both of us finishing up in a heap at the foot of the stairs.

Face contorted, the conductor came charging down the aisle. "You two again! I've a good mind to…!" The bus was midway between stops now, already slowing down, the clack-clack of the trolley arms crossing the points on the overhead lines. "If I catch you at that one more time it'll be your…! I'm warning you, I'll…!" He opened and bunched his fingers in frustration. In all the times I'd been on his bus I'd never known him to finish a sentence.

We scrambled up the stairs. Up on the top deck there were still plenty of empty seats and we made our way along the aisle to the front. As Gusty passed William he leaned across and flipped off his woollen hat onto the floor. I picked it up and handed it back.

Gusty dropped into the seat and slid across towards the window. I sat down beside him. The man across the aisle shook open the evening edition: *MOVE BY U.S. TO CURB CASTRO?* Gusty dug around in his jacket, pulled out a packet of Parkdrive and took one out. It was crumpled in the middle and he smoothed it straight, patted his pockets then leaned across

47

me and spoke to the man with the newspaper. "Got a match, mister?"

The man passed over a box and Gusty lit up, extracted a dozen or so matches then handed the box to me. I reached it back to the man. He went to put it in his pocket then held it up to his ear and shook it. A puzzled expression came over his face and he looked at me. I shrugged and he looked at the box again then put it back in his pocket and returned to his paper.

Behind us two men were holding an inquest on Saturday's fight: "It was Gilroy's from the start," said one.

"Caldwell didn't have the reach," said the other.

It started to rain again, the drops hitting the glass in front of us, smearing across and downwards to the rim.

Love Me Do playing on the transistor, a tinny sound. I guided the plane along the edge of the frame, the slivers curling and dropping to the floor. On the other side of the bench, William, like all first-year apprentices, was sanding doors. Near the entrance to the machine shop Ivan was hunched over, chiselling out dovetails for a drawer and behind me Mac, Jo-Jo and Michael were fitting together frames and stacking them against the wall.

The toilet flushed and Gusty came out, newspaper under his arm. "Where's Cuba?" he asked me.

"I'm not sure…Somewhere near America?"

"It's off the c-coast of Florida," said William. He dropped the sanding block, picked it up and as he straightened bumped against the door with his shoulder. It toppled over, sending up a cloud of sawdust while William hopped up and down holding his foot.

Gusty was first again. The overhead wires hummed as they swung and sparked in the moonlight. I hitched my knapsack round to my back and got ready.

The humming grew louder, the lights bigger, as the bus closed the distance. Gusty started running backwards. The front of the bus passed him and when the rear was almost level he reached for the bar and swung up onto the platform with the ease of a ballet dancer.

The bus came rushing towards me, trolleys clacking, points flashing, lights flickering as I started to back-pedal. The front passed me, wheels spinning close and the driver was screaming something and then the windows were flashing past, the faces goggling out at me. I grabbed the bar and skipped onto the platform, timing perfect, momentum swinging me round and clear of the road.

Gusty was halfway up the stairs and the conductor was halfway down the aisle. "You…! You…!"

I bounded up the steps, walked between the rows of seats, picked up William's hat and handed it to him. He pulled it down over his ears and slumped into his seat.

The man across from Gusty was opening his paper: *RUSSIANS HEAD FOR BLOCKADE.*

"Why shouldn't the Russians have missiles there? – The Yanks have had them in Turkey for years…So what's the difference? …Anyway, after last year can you blame Castro? – Hands off Cuba! Hands off Cuba!" Ivan was in full flow.

"What happened last year?" asked Gusty. I shrugged. Behind me William said something about pigs.

Ivan wasn't his real name. His real name was Bert but he had Communist leanings and would have liked nothing better than to be a shop steward. He paused, took a loud mouthful of tea; "Kennedy! Hah! I could tell you a thing or two about that fella – things would make your hair curl. I've a brother lives in America …You should hear the rumours goin' about." He set his mug on the bench. "There are stories about Kennedy and Marilyn, y'know…Marilyn Monroe. The way I hear it, it was very convenient she took that overdose." He swirled the tea in his mug and raised it to his lips, "Fella oughta be shot."

"Hey, Michael…Give us a drop of your milk." Gusty reached out his mug. "Our milkman didn't come this morning."

"Yer ma hasn't paid the bill, y'mean," said Jo-Jo.

"Paid the bill?" said Mac. "Where do you think Gusty got his red hair?"

Gusty lifted a handful of sawdust and poured it into Mac's mug. Mac jumped up with a curse and Gusty retreated round to the far side of the bench, jinking one way then the other, keeping the bench between them until Mac got short of breath. He put a hand to his chest and sat down again. Gusty, playing safe, stayed behind the bench.

"What's the latest, anyway?" asked Michael.

"Last I heard they were eyeballing each other," said Jo-Jo.

"Do you th-think it'll come to anything? Do you th-think there'll be a war?" asked William. He had a bandage round his thumb.

"I hope not," I said. "I don't fancy being called up."

"Called up? Called up for what?" shouted Ivan. "This wouldn't be the same as last time, y'know. This would be different…We're talkin' rockets and nuclear warheads here. Fire off a few of those and there'd be nothin' left to be called up for…or to, for that matter."

There was a long silence before William spoke again, clearly worried; "What should we do?"

Jo-Jo drained his mug, took a quick look round and lit a cigarette. On the wall behind him hung a sign; *NO SMOKING IN THE WORKSHOP.* "There's only one thing you can do."

"What's that?" asked William.

Jo-Jo leaned forward. "Well…You'll probably get a warning, see? – three minutes, about. This doesn't give you a lot of time so you need to be quick." He drew deeply on his cigarette, blew out a cloud of smoke. "What you do is – Soon as you hear the siren you try and make yourself as small as possible – that's very important – get under a table or under the stairs or something. Then bend over and hold your ankles and try and get your head as far between your knees as you can…" He paused, flicked the ash off his cigarette.

"And what do you do then?" asked William.

"And then you kiss your arse goodbye," said Jo-Jo.

There were loud hoots of laughter from the older men. I looked across at William but he wasn't laughing. He just sat there staring at the floor. Gusty had picked up a sanding block and was slowly drawing it back and forth along the edge of a window frame.

When the laughter died away William got up, collected the mugs and carried them over to the back door.

"What about Alf Ramsey, then…eh?" said Michael.

"About time, too…Maybe now we'll see some decent results."

I watched William as, one by one, he upended the mugs, spilling some of the dregs over his trousers. He didn't seem to notice, or maybe he didn't care. Head down, he turned away and stood there, motionless, silhouetted against the heavy greyness of the day.

The queue moved slowly. Our breath mingled with the fog drifting round our ears. Gusty had said he wasn't in the mood and to tell you the truth neither was I. A little ahead of us an old man with a walking stick was being urged along by a younger woman carrying two string shopping bags. There were four or five loaves of bread in each bag.

"Where's William?" I asked, looking along the queue.

"I don't know – He left just ahead of us. I saw him going out the door."

The man with the stick and the woman with the bread were on the bus now and the platform was slow in clearing as the others climbed on board. We just about managed to get on ourselves before somebody rang the bell.

For some reason the old man was insisting on going upstairs and the woman was trying to coax him out of the idea. Gusty was in front of me and I had barely enough room for my feet at the edge of the platform. I held on tightly to the bar as the bus moved off. The old man was stubbornly refusing to go into the lower deck.

We were picking up speed when I saw him some distance down the road, half hunched over, feet apart, the ridiculous little hat pulled down low on his forehead. I lost him for a moment in the swirl of the fog and then it cleared again. He had a determined look on his face.

"Aw, God...No!" I shouted. "Stop it! Stop the bus!" The old man and the woman were still arguing and we were all still crushed together on the platform. "No, William! No!" I yelled.

As we accelerated towards him he started to hop up and down. He stumbled, regained his balance and I heard the long blare of the horn as the front wheel narrowly missed his foot and then he was level with the platform and grabbing for the bar. I heard the slap as it hit his hand and then the momentum swept him off his feet leaving him half on, half hanging off the platform. His fingers started to slide down the bar. He tried to catch hold with his other hand but he was half turned towards the kerb and he couldn't get twisted back far enough. But he still held on, nearly horizontal now, his toecaps dragging along the surface of the road. Then Gusty was beside me. He dropped to his knees on the platform holding the bar with one hand. He swung out and caught William by the seat of the pants and at the same time I grabbed his arm. He was a dead weight. Gusty was shouting something but I couldn't hear him over the noise of the traffic and the screams from the passengers. Then the handle of a walking stick poked out past me and hooked into William's trouser belt. I heaved and William rolled onto the platform. We lay there in a tangle of legs and arms and knapsacks and over the screech of brakes as the bus shuddered to a halt I heard; "If that's those two again, I'll…! Let me past there till I get…!"

The old man with the walking stick turned to the woman. "See?" he said and stepped onto the stairs. The woman gave a sigh and went after him, shaking her head.

William's face was red with the exertion and his breath came in great whooping gasps. Blood was seeping through a tear in the knee of his trousers and his shoes were ruined but he stood there grinning at us, his hat hanging off one ear. Gusty reached out and straightened it.

"I warned you, didn't …! Didn't I tell you if you ever…!" The conductor was standing behind us poking his finger in the air. "That's it!…I'm going to…!" He stopped. Gusty was holding out a ten-bob note. The conductor looked at him, he looked at me and he looked at William and his hand went to the machine at his waist and he punched out three tickets and gave them to Gusty. Without a word he thumbed the change into Gusty's hand then stood to one side to let us past. We were part way up the stairs when he called to us; "Hey, you three!" I turned and looked down at him. There was no longer anger in his eyes. Then he said, "I used to be young… wondering what was coming… I can remember how it was." And he rang the bell and stepped back into the downstairs aisle as the bus lurched into motion.

Upstairs we walked between the rows of seats, William, limping, leading the way. "Bloody eejits," somebody said as we went past. Up at the front of the bus William slid into the window seat and Gusty sat down beside him. I got into the seat behind and leaned forward between them, my elbows on the backrest.

Gusty brought out his cigarettes and offered one to William. William shook his head. He was still smiling.

The man across the aisle was half-turned in his seat, arms spread, reading the inside pages. The headline said: *BLOCKADE AN ACT OF WAR, SAYS CUBA.*

Gusty straightened a cigarette, put it in his mouth. He made no attempt to light it and we sat there, the three of us, not saying anything, swaying slightly with the movement of the bus.

We rounded the bend and laboured up towards the bridge, the pens of the cattle mart, deserted now, spread out below and over to our left. We crossed the river and swept down the other side towards the junction of the roads. Still no one spoke. Ahead of me I could see, as I had seen every time I had made that journey since I was a child, the words, red and blue neon, diffused through the fog, flashing in steady sequence, in synchrony with the clack, clack of the overhead trolleys as they crossed the points: *DON'T BE VAGUE...ASK FOR HAIG.....DON'T BE VAGUE...ASK FOR HAIG........*

AZALEAS

I am a sceptic. I don't believe in premonitions or visitations or karma or any of that stuff. I believe there is a rational explanation for everything that happens in life. It all comes down to logic.

But sometimes.....

It was nine years old with rusting wheel arches and all I could afford then, hardly a week passing but something needed replaced or adjusted or tightened. It was early April, I remember, and my back ached from leaning across the wing trying to loosen the alternator bolt. Without the right kind of spanner I'd burred the angles off the bolt head and, in spite of the chill of the evening, sweat was running into my eyes, my knuckles were skinned and bleeding and that was when he appeared at my side.

"What's the problem?" He rested a hand on my shoulder, leaning past me, peering into the engine compartment.

I looked at the misshapen bolt head, the rusty spanner, the blood welling from my knuckles and I said, "Problem? There's no problem. There's nothing I like better than getting my hands covered in dirt and grease and blood. In fact, Dad, I'm thinking of doing a week-end of this sometime. I might even take the Friday off, make an early start, y'know?"

He took his hand from my shoulder. He stood on a moment then turned and walked back down the path to where he had been working at the flowerbeds. He picked up the pruners and the garden fork, went over to the shed, wiped them with a rag and set them inside. He closed the door, slid the bolt across, turned the key in the padlock. Then he came walking back past me and climbed the steps towards the house.

"Dad?" I said.

I collected the spanners, the screwdrivers, the oil, the blood-stained handkerchief and set them aside, dropped the bonnet, leaned my elbows on it and watched the sun going down.

By the time I went inside he'd gone. Some excuse about not feeling hungry and wanting an early night, he'd set off right away to walk the two miles to the station.

Why am I telling you this? I'm telling you because he died three days later before I got around to saying I was sorry, before the azaleas began to bloom.

My father had two interests in life. In his younger days he'd played football – amateur league stuff, making the headlines once in the local press when he scored a hat trick – back in the fifties long before I was born. After my mother died I'd made a point of calling a couple of times a week to make sure he was eating properly, taking his medication, that kind of thing. He'd sit in his chair by the fire and talk about the game, the way it had got to be, the way it was then. "No individuality anymore," he would say…"all they do now is play to a pattern. Where are all the Dohertys and Wrights these days, eh? – All the Lofthouses and Matthews's? – Tell me that."

And, of course, I couldn't. Mainly because I hadn't the slightest interest. I remember him taking me to the park, I couldn't have been any more than five, the old dun-coloured ball under his arm, and all I'd wanted to do was chase the ducks.

His interest in the garden had started in later years, around the time I got married and mortgaged myself to the hairline on a house set in a quarter acre. I was more than happy to let him dig and plant and prune until he'd transformed it into a landscape of colour, a vegetable patch for good measure. It was the previous autumn that he'd planted the azalea bush at the bottom of the garden near the fence line and close to the silver birch.

The morning he died I was on my way south for an early appointment. I had risen at five-thirty and it was still dark when I leaned across the bed and kissed Elaine on the cheek. I tip-toed into the children's bedrooms and listened for a moment to their soft breathing. Then I slipped out and was on the motorway by six-fifteen.

I called home from a filling station around eight o'clock to make sure everyone was awake and the line was engaged. When I rang again an hour later from a roadside café Elaine told me through the sobs that my father had died during the night. And I stood there holding the phone, the background smell of bacon and coffee, and all I could see was the hurt on an old man's face in the fading light of an April evening when I should have known better.

It started a couple of months ago. Well, that's not quite right, for the image, that last look on my father's face, had been with me on and off for the twelve years or so since he died. Most of the time I'd be free of it. Then, without any trigger of association, no matter where I was or what I was doing I would feel it coming at me and I would re-run the whole thing in my head.

Early April once more and I was fixing the catch on the gate when I became aware of the stillness. When a moment before there had been the shouts of the children next door, the sound of the radio from the kitchen, the drone of an aeroplane, there was an absolute silence. For some reason I looked round at the azalea bush. Then, as suddenly as they had stopped, the sounds of normality returned.

I slept badly after that, waking in the early hours when he would walk into my dreams, the hurt plain on his face. Elaine voiced her concern more than once but I got round it by saying I was having problems with the book. I knew she didn't believe me, of course, but she didn't push it.

Spring rolled over into early summer and the days grew long and the grass lush and the azaleas bloomed into colour and then this rain came.

It hasn't stopped for over a week now, a steady, misty rain that lies like a web on your clothes and dampens your spirit. I have mooched around the house, unable to discipline myself to get on with the book, starting minor household repairs, leaving them half done and moving on to something else, every now and then looking out of the window at the garden, praying for a change in the weather.

It's now the evening of the second wet Saturday and to my relief the rain clouds are drifting towards the east and there is a widening brightness in the sky. The water is lying in a pool on the patio and I am trying to figure how I can improve the drainage when I see him.

I don't know how long he's been there, well back in the shadow of the silver birch, and as I step closer to the window he comes slowly out into the open and stands there looking around.

He is the way I always remember him – tall, thinning white hair and that tanned skin, even in winter, that we always envied. I suppose I have been expecting him for some time now. I open the door and step out onto the patio and into the silence. A little hesitatingly I walk across the wet grass to meet him, the soft breeze tugging my sleeves.

When I am a little way from him I stop. He is leaning over the azaleas, examining them. I want to reach out.

He looks up. "Son? Is that you?" He comes closer, those bright grey eyes squinting in the low, weak sun. "Why…I expected…You look….."

"Older?"

"Yes…Older." He seems a little wistful.

"You look the way I want you to look."

He turns, nodding to himself, taking everything in. "You have a nice place. The garden's not the way I remember it though." He points over towards the far edge of the patio; "There used to be a sandpit there."

"I filled it in. The children are grown up now."

"Children?…Oh, yes – the children. How are they? The boy…Gosh, I've forgotten his name, it's so long ago."

"Jonathan."

"Ah, of course…Jonathan…He had a patch over one eye."

"A lazy muscle. He grew out of it. He's at university."

"University? Well, isn't that something…And the little girl… Christine?"

"Working in Edinburgh…a children's hospital."

He smiles, that old familiar smile. "My, my…And Elaine…How is Elaine?"

"She's well. She's in the house but…but as you're only in my…"

"In your mind?" He nods, "Maybe I am…Maybe I am."

Strange, but for some reason I can't tell what he's wearing. I try to remember what he used to wear. What had he on that last day? A worn pair of trousers, most likely – and a pullover and a zip-up jacket to keep out the chill.

"Dad?" I say.

"Yes?"

"There's something I need to make right because I never got the chance before you…before you went but I don't know how because I can't find the words…" I reach out my hands in frustration. "Look at me! – a writer and I can't find the words!"

"A writer? You've become a writer?" He chuckles. "You always were one for the books. The other kids couldn't wait to get onto the street to kick a ball about, but you…you could always be found with your nose buried in a book." He shakes his head in wonder. "My son a writer." He looks around him again. "The azaleas – they've taken a beating."

"The rain…there's been a lot of rain."

He gestures at the flowerbeds, the shrubs, the lawn. "I always loved this garden."

I hear sounds, faint, as if through a vacuum – birds, music, the shouts of children. I have only moments now. "Wait…Don't go yet."

"But I have to."

"Can't you stay a little while?"

"But my time's nearly gone…I only have a short while."

"Will you come back?"

He shakes his head; "No…I don't think so. You don't need me in your life anymore, cluttering it up. It's best this way. Anyhow, I'm not sure I'd want to come back…I wouldn't fit, you see." He is fading.

Say it quickly – Now's the time. "Wait…That day…the day I was fixing the car, remember? I treated you badly. I said something – something I didn't mean… I was unfair and… I'm sorry."

He looks at me, those clear grey eyes. "So that's why you brought me back." He smiles. "It's so long ago…I'd forgotten about it to tell you the truth…Anyway, it's okay…apology accepted." Then he isn't smiling anymore. "You and me…we never said the important things. But that didn't mean…" He pauses. "You know what I'm trying to say?"

"Yes." I am a child again.

"Well, then," he straightens his shoulders… "Can't we just leave it that way?"

I nod. My throat is tight.

He sighs. "Time to go... Take care of Elaine and the...I nearly said the children...but they're not anymore, are they?" I make to speak, but he continues; "I wish I'd been around to see them grow." He looks down at the azalea bush. "Seems I missed all the growing." He turns to me; "Well... so long, then... Maybe you'll write about me sometime, eh?"

I nod. "I promise."

He backs away, raises his hand, walks slowly down the path. As he passes the azalea bush he stops a moment and gently touches one of the flowers.

And then he is gone.

I am conscious of the sounds of dusk. The trees sigh, a dog barks somewhere. From the kitchen behind me I hear the gravelly voice of Chris Rea... wasted lifetimes...

The back door bursts open and the ball, white, black pentagons, bounces onto the patio, ricochets past me and down across the lawn.

"It's over, Dad – the rain's over at last."

I turn and look at him.

My son is eight years old and growing an inch a day. He is wearing a tee shirt hanging out at one side of his shorts. His hair is soft and fair like his mother's and his eyes are a clear shade of grey I've only ever seen once before. He is a latecomer and spoilt rotten by his brother and sister when they are home. His name is David – after his grandfather. He wants to be a professional footballer and he says he is going to play for Aston Villa. I wouldn't be at all surprised. They changed their kit this past season and it's going to cost me seventy quid in September when his birthday comes around. Already he plays in the school team with boys three and four years older.

He jumps off the patio and runs after the ball. "What were you looking at just now? – You were standing there for ages."

"Just the azaleas," I say.

He reaches the ball and turns and my father speaks to me; "World Cup," he says.

My son places the sole of his foot on the ball and flips it back and hooks it into the air. He starts to kick it with alternate feet, at all times keeping it clear of the grass. Faster he goes, the ball spinning higher and higher.

World Cup. The World Cup is almost a year and two thousand miles away. I could put off changing the car and I have a little money in the building society and there's the life endowment. It's not due to mature for another three years but three years is too long and there are things to be done. I'll lose a bit by cashing it in early but I'm doing mental arithmetic now and I know Elaine will say to go for it and my son is heading the ball in the air, his forehead getting blacker by the second.

"Fancy a kick about?" he shouts. He lets the ball drop, traps it, stands there, left foot on top, hands on hips, big wide smile.

"Okay, Dad," I say.

"What was that?" asks my son.

"Nothing." I will ring the insurance company first thing in the morning. I lean forward, legs apart.

He lobs the ball towards me. It is going to pass well to my left. I launch myself sideways arms outstretched and catch it. I fall onto the grass, the ball slippery in my hands. I roll and push myself up. My shirt is soaking wet and my shoulder hurts but I am laughing and so is my son. I overarm the ball to him and he leans back, deflects it downwards with his chest, traps it with his left instep, nudges it sideways... all in one flow of movement.

The daylight fades. It is dusk. I hear the leaves whisper in the trees as he kicks the ball towards me. I kick it back. He kicks it to me again. I kick it back.

SOUP OF THE DAY

Mrs Johnston didn't like the soup.

Nor did she like the carrots, the gravy, the pork escallops. In fact, if you want to be all inclusive, she didn't like the table cloth, the table location, the wine and just about everything else since she and Mr Johnston had stepped through the doorway of Lester's Brasserie.

Mr Johnston didn't like Mrs Johnston.

It hadn't always been that way. When they had met and for the first few years, back in the days when he and she were young, Maggie, passions erupted like volcanoes, hormones raged against the dying of the light.

But that was a lifetime ago and now that Mrs Johnston's hair was frizzy and her skin had started to pucker and her bosom was moving exponentially nearer the earth's core Mr Johnston had lost all semblance of interest.

Mandy Murphy's bosom was not moving nearer the earth's core. No, Sirree! Mandy Murphy's *embonpoint* was the talk of the restaurant and her *derriere* (now we're in French mode) could not have been better designed for pushing open the double spring doors into the kitchen, especially those times when her arms, from wrist to forearm, were hidden under layers of soup dishes, dinner plates and casseroles. I tell you, *mon ami*, she was the sole focus of attention of the eyes of all male diners between the ages of fourteen and eighty-four.

Mr Johnston, who was not fourteen and furthermore was not eighty-four, liked Mandy Murphy. That's why he and Mrs Johnston were dining in Lester's for the fourth night in a row – ever since Mr Johnston first clapped his beady eyes on her.

Mandy Murphy didn't like Mr Johnston. Mandy Murphy could pick out a groper at a hundred paces.

At this precise moment Mr Johnston wasn't a hundred paces away. In fact he was about three feet away and well within striking distance. He waited for his chance.

Mandy Murphy placed the dessert in front of Mrs Johnston who immediately frowned and leaned over to poke at a slice of pineapple in her fritter. She picked up her fork and turned over the pineapple to inspect the underside. She paused, looked up at Mandy Murphy and pointed.

Mandy Murphy bent across the table to see what Mrs Johnston was about to complain about this time and Mr Johnston, three days in the planning, made his move. His hand, out of Mrs Johnston's line of vision, glided round the side of the table.

Mandy Murphy liked kick-boxing. Second Dan at her local dojo, her reaction was swift and uncompromising, her aim laser true.

Mr Johnston, now divorced from Mrs Johnston, never fully recovered. He lives quietly in a Benedictine retreat near the foot of the Sperrin Mountains. He can occasionally be seen in the nearby town where he is instantly recognisable by the funny way he walks. He is wary of big girls.

Mandy Murphy has now attained the level of Third Dan. Having saved enough tips from her admiring customers to open her own dojo (pensioners half price on Wednesdays) she can now pick out a groper at a hundred and fifty paces.

Mrs Johnston lives in a state of near euphoria with a twenty-two year old Algerian exchange student with an Oedipus complex and a *penchant* for Mexican cuisine. She can't get enough of his tostadas.

SIGNS OF RAIN

Belfast, 1949

Mrs McAllister had been in and out several times, scurrying between the two houses as the afternoon wore on. Around six o'clock her oldest girl had set off on her bicycle and not long afterwards the tall woman, the boy had never seen her before, a large bag over her shoulder, knocked on the door and Mrs McAllister let her in. She carried out a whispered conversation with the tall woman, then turned to the boy and suggested, now that she had made him his dinner, he go outside and watch for his father coming home.

The boy, glad of an excuse to get away from whatever was happening, but no less worried, nodded and went out, passing the neat stack of towels on the table near the window.

Throughout the afternoon his mother, upstairs now in the front of the two bedrooms, had, from time to time, taken a sharp breath, quickly recovering her composure and smiling over at him reassuringly. When he thought she wasn't looking he would glance over the top of his comic to see if she was all right.

Now, hunkered down, back against the front wall of the house, he considered for a moment setting out to meet his father but sometimes the lorry would drop him off and he could come in by any one of three different ways and be easily missed.

An empty cigarette packet pirouetted at the kerb edge. There had been an occasional slight gust of wind since mid-day and the blue sky of the past two weeks was gradually being replaced by clouds, white at first, darkening now. Across towards the far side of the street the wet patch where the breadman's horse had relieved itself was almost completely dried out, the pungent smell fading. Now and then a door would open and a head would pop out, the face would turn towards his house for a moment and disappear again. Somewhere a radio played swing.

He poked a finger down the insides of his gutties, took them off one at a time and adjusted the pieces of cardboard covering the hole in each sole. He heard the heavy tread of Mrs McAllister's feet on the stairs. He hoped his father would come home soon.

It was so gradual he wasn't aware of it right away. It came from beyond the next row of houses, the longest and busiest of the maze of streets that made up the neighbourhood, a distant sound of shouting. It was a while before he could make out the words: "Fight!...Fight!..."

He jumped up, looked round at his front door, then up towards the top end of the street where people were now hurrying past, the shouting louder: "Fight!...Fight!...Fight!..." Over the noise of the voices he heard a distant rumble of thunder.

He started to run. Doors opened as he passed and other footsteps sounded behind him as he rounded the corner. Over by the waste ground near the mission hall a crowd had gathered. He raced towards it, circled it, tried to find a way through. "Who is it?" someone called out.

"Who do you think it is?" somebody else replied.

The boy dodged to one side then the other, ducked his head and burrowed his way through the shifting mass of bodies and legs. By the time he squirmed to the centre of the ring the first blood had been shed. He stumbled as he broke free and someone grabbed him before he could fall and pulled him out of the way.

In front of him Matt Brown moved ponderously, turning in a half-circle, big fists flailing wildly in the hope that one would connect and bring the fight to a swift end as indeed it would have.

Danny Weir darted in, feinted a body punch with his right fist, twisted slightly and followed with a jab to Matt Brown's cheek. He danced back, dabbing at the cut on his bottom lip.

The crowd, men and boys mostly, a woman here and there, shouted at the two youths, egging them on as they warily circled one another. From the direction of the mission hall a wheezy organ started up and the boy heard singing: "Shall we gather at the river… the beautiful, the beautiful river…"

Behind the boy someone asked what started it. One of the women piped up; "Sure the two families have been at it for years. They only have to pass each other in the street for it to start up. They were at it before the war and it's still goin' on…Here's yer man – Here's Enoch now."

The boy looked round. The crowd was parting to allow the man through, buttoning his trousers, pulling his braces over his shoulders as he came. The boy had seen him before but not this close, a huge man, a fringe of black, oiled hair above his ears. He stopped, hooked his thumbs in his waistband and made as though to call his son over, then a look of recognition came over his face. He nodded a couple of times then; "Go ahead, Matt…Give it to him… Good and hard." Enoch Brown pushed up his shirtsleeves, exposing massive tattooed forearms, and leant forward.

His son, reluctantly it seemed to the boy, moved towards Danny Weir, fists extended, reach longer, superior strength obvious. Danny Weir skipped in, ducked quickly under Matt's arms jabbed him in the stomach and followed through with a hard punch to his chin.

"Gather with the saints at the river… that flows …"

The boy had never seen anything like this before. He felt a mixture of exhilaration and guilt. He knew his mother and father wouldn't want him there.

Enoch Brown yelled at his son to keep moving forward, to take the fight to his opponent; "You're not goin' to let that trash do that to you! Give him one! – Just one! – That's all it'll take!" Those nearest him moved away, opening up a space.

The boy had heard the rumours – something about the war and a German prisoner and a dishonourable discharge. He sensed the brutality of the man. His own father wouldn't have been much younger and he, too, had been in the war, but the boy never heard him talk about it.

"Yes, we will gather at the river…"

The sky was dark overhead now and little swirls of dust rose from the surface of the road. Danny Weir moved in again, weaving under Matt Brown's wild swings and landed another punch to Matt's cheek. The bigger youth was moving slowly now, his breathing heavy. His father continued to urge him on; "Come on, boy! – Go after the skitter!" But it was clear that Matt was tiring. The smaller, lighter, nimbler Danny looked like he could go on forever, constantly moving, landing quick, accurate punches that were taking their toll on the overweight Matt. Enoch Brown knew, the boy could see it in his eyes, the clenching of his jaw. He felt a strange rush of pity for the man as he watched his son take the steady beating.

Matt stumbled and lost his balance and Danny moved in to finish it. But he didn't get far. Enoch lunged out and grabbed him, pinning his arms to his sides. There was a collective howl of protest and a couple of the men moved forward but stopped short. Danny was wriggling trying to free himself. He kicked upwards but there was no escaping Enoch's bear hug.

The crowd went quiet. After a moment Danny stopped struggling and hung there, his feet just off the ground. The singing in the mission hall ended and the boy could hear the raised intonation of prayer but couldn't make out the words. Enoch Brown spoke, his voice low; "OK, Matt...Hit him...Hit him hard."

Matt looked round. A woman whimpered as he stepped in front of Danny. "Go ahead, son...I'll hold him," said Enoch. Danny, arms pinned back, looked straight into Matt's eyes as Matt punched him in the mouth. A woman screamed as blood spurted out of Danny's mouth and splashed onto the front of his shirt. He was still looking straight at Matt.

"Aw, Jasus," said the man beside the boy. He turned and pushed his way out through the crowd. Another man followed. Then another.

The door of the mission hall groaned open and people began to emerge, women mostly, wearing hats, a few men in worn, dark suits and sombre ties. Some of them looked over at the scene then hurried away up the street, glancing back, murmuring as they did so. There was another rumble of thunder, close now.

Enoch let go and Danny took an unsteady pace towards Matt. Matt dropped his head, stared at the ground, arms hanging by his side. Danny stood there a moment, fist raised. Then he shook his head and turned and walked away from the other youth and through the slowly-dispersing crowd, shoulders hunched, hand cupped over his mouth.

Matt stepped around his father, his head lowered. As he did so Enoch reached out but Matt brushed his hand aside and stumbled down the street towards his home.

Enoch stood there watching the people, searching their faces as they turned their backs and one by one walked away until, apart from the boy, the street was deserted. There was a loud slam and the rattle of keys. The boy looked round. As always, Mr Redpath, the preacher, wore a black jacket and grey pinstripe trousers. His white shirt collar was starched rigid, his tie minutely knotted. He pulled his homburg a little more squarely on his head and turned, noticing Enoch.

Enoch hadn't moved. The two men faced each other across the piece of waste ground. The sky was heavy now, oppressive. Enoch spoke; "But he's my son, you see."

Mr Redpath tucked his bible firmly under one arm and his face broke into a Steradent smile. "Praise the lord, brother," he said and turned and strode smartly up the street with a rhythmic swing of his umbrella.

Enoch watched the preacher till he reached the top of the street and disappeared from sight, then turned towards the boy. There was no one else left now and all the doors were closed. Enoch held out both hands towards him, palms up as if to catch the coming rain. His lips moved but the words were drowned out by another rattle of thunder, overhead now.

The boy stepped back a few paces and started to run. He turned the corner into his own street. Down near the far end a man was coming towards him, a tall man, thin, walking quickly and the boy ran all the faster on seeing him for even at that distance he could see the smile on his father's face.

In those days, there was nothing particularly sinister about family men patrolling their neighbourhoods to protect their hearth and home.
Peter Taylor, *Loyalists.*

HEARTH AND HOME

Belfast, 1970

Anytime he'd gone over in the past few weeks it had been during the daylight hours and he hadn't noticed much out of the ordinary. Tonight, turning off the main road into the enclave of narrow streets, he had a sense of things changed, a barrier coming down.

Over towards the glass factory doorway a half dozen or so men were standing just out of range of the street lamp. One of them detached himself from the others and stepped onto the road. Robert was blinded for a moment by the sudden beam from a flashlight, but not before he caught the glint of something lying across the surface of the road. He braked sharply, closed his eyes, turned his head away, the circle of light trapped in his retinas.

The man rapped his side window. Robert wound it down a few inches and the flashlight beam swept across the passenger seat, jerking in towards the rear. Then it shone again in his face. He blinked, raised his arm.

"Sorry, Bobby…Didn't know it was you." The flashlight went off. "How's it goin'?" asked Kenny McCracken.

Robert rubbed his eyes and squinted up. Kenny wore a woollen watch cap, his collar pulled up against the cold February night. "What's all this?" Robert nodded across towards the group of men back now in the shadow of the gateway.

Kenny shrugged. "Well… everybody's kind of scared at the minute with all that's goin' on. We got together…all of us …decided we'd set up –" He stopped as another car turned into the street. He ducked down, moving back so that Robert's car was between him and the newcomer. There was movement over in the shadows. Kenny fumbled with the flashlight, switched it on, pointed it at the other car. "Talk to you again, Bobby." He edged warily past.

Robert raised a hand in acknowledgement and eased forward, seeing the glint again as the plank, rows of nails protruding, slid out of his path. It was then he noticed the other two men, one each side of the street, each holding the end of a length of rope. He passed them and in his rear-view mirror saw the plank being dragged back into place.

He drove on past the sub-station with its green metal palisade, past the scout hall, past the little Elim Mission and round the corner into the street where he had been born, thinking all the while – if I was ever in any doubt before, I'm in no doubt now.

He switched off the engine and sat a moment. On the journey over he'd tried to think of the best way to tell them. Should he just come straight out with it? Should he maybe wait a bit, tell them when he thought the moment was right?

He got out and locked the car. The heavy outer door was pulled tight, the hall light shining out through the oval transom. He looked up, then down the street. All the other outer doors were similarly closed. He remembered the time when this would have been unheard of, all the doors open, a welcome to all. His breath misting round his face he selected the key by feel and slipped it into the lock.

Inside, he went along the narrow hallway, glancing into the tiny front parlour, its three-piece moquette suite almost filling the room, the irritating nasal sound of Hughie Greene on the other side of the rear living-room door. He opened it and poked his head in. "Hello, Mum."

She'd been dozing. She jerked upright, hand fluttering to her chest, "Oh, Lord, Robert – you made me jump." The ball of wool dropped from her lap and rolled across the floor. She made a grab for the needles and the part-finished sleeve.

There was a burst of applause and the clapometer pointer swung through seventy degrees. "Turn that off," said his mother. "I only had it on for the company."

He switched off the television and sat down. "Where's Dad, then?"

She rolled her eyes. "He's vigilante-ing."

"He's what?"

"He's vigilante-ing – Up at the main road. Did you not see him?"

"I came in at the other end…There were men stopping cars…You mean he's with them?"

"When he heard about it he said he'd do his bit…They told him they didn't want him…Said he was a bit on the old side – you can imagine how that went down."

Robert stood. "I'm going up to bring him back. He shouldn't be standing up there – he's just got over the 'flu, for God's sake."

"Well, maybe he'll listen to you… you know what he's like, stubborn oul fool. He won't heed a word I say."

He turned the corner into the long dark street that joined both main roads, walking quickly, hunched over against the cold. A group of youths stood at the edge of the stretch of waste ground where the car workshop used to be.

…A week…We need to know inside a week. This is a great opportunity for you, Robert…a better career path…and, need we say, better money. You'd be foolish not to take it – but we have to know this week……

As he passed the shop he glanced in. Malachy had opened a carton of sweets and was stacking the packets on the shelf behind the counter. He looked the way he'd always looked – the immaculate tan overall coat, the blue shirt and tie, hair like it had been trimmed the day before. When his wife had died a couple of years ago most of the neighbourhood, those who could get off that was, were at the chapel, those who couldn't making a point of sending a mass card. Tonight Malachy wore a worried frown.

Robert tugged up his collar. A car approached him from behind, slowing as it drew level. He looked round. Four faces peered out at him, one, the front passenger, familiar in the half-light. He said something to the driver and the car picked up speed again.

...A better life. Ah, but it sounded good. I'll never get an offer like this again. Problem is them wanting me to go right away. Maybe if I hold out they'll pay for my flights back at weekends until I find somewhere. Rachel will be leaving work in a couple of months anyway – it won't be all that long. I mean, if they're that keen they should be prepared to facilitate me, shouldn't they? Meantime I can be looking for a place... But will Rachel be all right during the week? And should she be involved in a move right now? Isn't it supposed to be risky?... The more he thought about it, the more uncertain he became.

The car of a minute ago had stopped near the top of the street. Here, too, a group of men stood in the shadows, a plank like before lying across the road. He tried to pick out his father.

One of the men left the shadows and walked across to the car, leaning forward. He turned and beckoned towards the group. Another man walked over, hesitant. Robert, close enough now, recognised Jerome.

He spotted his father then, scarf wrapped high around his neck, cap pulled low, hands in his pockets, the old army greatcoat that had been his grandfather's – long, coarse cloth, heavy. It used to hang on the hook on the inside of Robert's bedroom door. Robert recalled the big snowfall of 1948, his father coming into his bedroom one night, laying the coat across the top of the bedclothes, spreading it out, moulding it round him, the old comforting smell of whatever its pockets used to hold.

He heard raised voices. The front-seat passenger was thrusting something out towards Jerome and Jerome was shaking his head, backing away.

Robert's father walked across to the car and spoke to the passenger. He sounded angry. Jerome was getting more agitated. Always the timid one, Jerome, since as far back as Robert could remember. Like the time they camped out under a cover of potato sacking on the far side of the allotments and, of all things, a fox ran past them. They'd never before seen a live one and Matt, Tommy and he had thrown sticks and chased it. It easily outdistanced them. Jerome had said it was probably hungry and he felt sorry for it.

Matt, his brother Tommy, Jerome, Robert. Football against the goalmouth chalked on the gable wall in winter. Cricket in the summer against wickets chalked on the same wall. Footprints left forever on the fresh cement the time they re-did the road. The footprints were still there, the goalmouth and the wickets gone, the wall too. And Tommy.

Robert's father hadn't seen him approach. He was still arguing with the man in the car. Robert looked in at Matt, different now – hair long, sideburns down nearly to his chin, dark Zapata moustache. He was holding something wrapped in a paper bag, still thrusting it at Jerome.

Robert's father started to cough, hard, painful. He doubled over, turned away. Robert ran forward and grabbed him, held him by the elbow, other arm at the older man's back as he fought for air, a long whooping sound.

After a minute the coughing eased and his father's breathing steadied. He looked at Robert. "What are you doing here tonight? You don't usually…" His eyes searched Robert's. "There's nothing wrong, is there? Rachel…Is Rachel all right?"

"Rachel's fine, Dad… Everything's okay."

The car engine revved and Robert turned. Matt spoke from the passenger seat, "Well, well, Bobby – Down from the leafy suburbs to see how the other half's surviving?"

Friends. We were friends once, thought Robert. "Hello, Matt…Sorry to hear about Tommy."

Matt looked at him, dismissed him, turned his head away and spoke to the driver. The car moved off with a jerk and pulled out onto the main road.

Jerome stood watching it. He was holding something inside his coat and he was shaking. "You okay, Jerome?" asked Robert and Jerome nodded, still staring at the main road long after the car was gone.

"You know what they gave Jerome, don't you?"

They were halfway down the street. His father, a brisk walker as a rule, had slowed down a bit as winter took its toll. Robert felt a rush of regret and a sudden awareness of the passage of time. He nodded. "Yes…I know what it was."

"It could have been you instead of Jerome if you hadn't moved away," said his father.

It could have been me instead of Matt, thought Robert…or Tommy.

"Rachel keeping all right, then?"

"Yes…She's all right – a bit sick in the mornings, though." As they passed each house he caught the television flicker through the gaps in the curtains.

They neared the bottom of the street. Malachy was brushing splinters of glass out onto the pavement and one of the panels in the door was shattered. The group of youths was nowhere to be seen.

They crossed over towards the shop. Malachy disappeared inside and came back out with a dustpan. He saw them approach and bent down to scoop up the glass. His finger was bleeding.

"What's all this, Malachy?" asked Robert's father. "What happened?"

Malachy was slow to reply. "Well you couldn't say it was an accident." He looked down the street.

"Did you see who it was? Tell me and I'll make sure the parents know."

"I didn't see."

Robert knew it wasn't true. Malachy took the hand brush and swept up the remaining debris.

"I'll help you board it up," said Robert's father.

Malachy shook his head. He looked at his finger, as if only now aware of the cut. He wiped it on the front of the tan overall. "I don't need any help." He looked around him; "Thirty-two years next month – that's how long I've been here." He went back inside the shop, closing the door.

Robert's father stood there a moment then walked on. Robert hung back, looking in through the window. Malachy was rummaging under the counter.

It wasn't hard to catch up. "That's the way it begins," said the older man. "With little things – Like a pane of glass." As they rounded the corner Robert heard the sound of hammering behind him.

His father spoke again, low; "I remember…It was a long time ago…I was young… seventeen or so. It was July and we'd all just started back to the shipyard after the twelfth fortnight. There were going to be changes… big ones…political, that is…

"There'd been a meeting during the dinner hour. A lot of hotheads… a lot of speeches. One thing led to another and then a crowd, must have been five hundred or more, started through the yards, waving Union Jacks, carrying sticks. I was one of them.

"We ordered them out – the Catholics. Some of them resisted. We … encouraged… them and eventually chased them out.

"But we couldn't even leave it at that. We went after them, trapped them with their backs to the channel. Some jumped in…and the rest we threw in… Some tried to wade back out. We were waiting for them with pockets filled with rivets.

"There was this one fellow – around my age. I knew him to see about the place. I'd have nodded to him and he'd have nodded to me…Every time he tried to get out I pushed him back till after a while he just stood there, water up to his waist.

"By that time most of them had either swum across to the other side or waded far enough along to get away so there were just the two of us. He was shaking with the cold, his arms wrapped round himself… He started to cry….." His father stopped suddenly, his head down. Robert waited.

"I can see her yet… this young girl. She had long black hair, down past her shoulders, and she was wearing a white dress. A wedding dress of all things. Why she was wearing it I'll never know, but she was so…" He was silent for a moment… "She took my breath away…..

"She walked past me into the water and out to the man. She put her arm round him, helped him out. He could hardly walk. She led him past me and as she did so she looked straight through me like I wasn't there…..

"When I got back to the machine shop they cheered me and slapped me on the back. The manager came out into the shop…A big noise in the Orange Order, I remember. He walked over to me, looked me up and down and he said; 'A job well done, lad? – I suppose you think you can call yourself a man, now?' I turned and walked out of the shop and never went back…It was the look on her face – I keep seeing it."

He took a deep breath, started walking again. "He hasn't a chance, Malachy. He'll carry on for a while – a couple of weeks – a month, maybe, but…there's not a thing we'll be able to do. People like Matt – they'll be the ones with the power… and they'll wall up peoples' minds. I've seen it before but there's worse coming.…..You've been looking at you shoes."

"What?" Robert stopped. They were outside the house.

"You were looking all the time at your shoes – you used to do that when you were a kid and something was troubling you."

"No…No…There's nothing troubling me…" His father was looking at him – a steady look. Then he nodded slowly.

The hall light was off. "Your mother was going across to see Mrs McCartney – she must be away," said his father. "We could both use a hot cup of tea."

"I can't stay. I'd better get back to Rachel – I told her I wouldn't be too long."

"So you didn't come round for any particular reason, then?"

"No…No particular reason…Just…" Robert became conscious he was looking down at his shoes again. He quickly raised his head. There was an awkward silence.

"Bad times," said his father. Down the street a door slammed and a dark shape shuffled towards the corner, a grotesque shadow on the wall as it passed the street lamp. "It's the children I feel sorry for – It's not going to be much of a place to grow up in."

Robert swallowed. He didn't know the right words and all he wanted to do was reach out but that had never been his father's way.

"Don't leave it too long…" his father paused. Robert looked at him. He knows…

"…until you call round again," his father finished.

He turned the corner. A square of plywood was nailed across Malachy's door. Robert slowed and stopped. Inside Malachy took off his tan overall, tossed it across the counter. He reached behind the door into the back store, lifted out his overcoat, searched in the pockets. Robert wondered if he should offer him a lift but decided he would probably be met with a rebuff. He drove off again.

As he neared the top of the street the nailed plank slid to one side. Jerome was standing apart from the other men. He was shivering, one hand in his topcoat pocket, the other tight across his midriff as though this gave him a degree of comfort. He looked nervously at the car as it stopped beside him. Robert lowered the window and spoke across; "Don't allow them to do this, Jerome. It doesn't have to be this way."

"It's not that easy, Bobby." Jerome blinked rapidly behind his glasses. "My ma … She's lived here all her life and won't leave and… she depends on me… What can I do?"

If Robert had had an answer he'd have given it. He nodded; "I think I know…" One of the other men was looking over at them. "Be careful, Jerome…Be careful." He raised a hand and pulled slowly away.

Clouds were starting to build up overhead and he could smell the coming rain as he wound up the window. He drove past the nailed plank and before turning out onto the main road glanced in his mirror. Jerome was standing there, well away from the other men and it might just have been the angle of vision but it seemed to Robert he had the look of a fox, out of open space, backed into a corner, nowhere to run, no place left to hide.

TOO TIRED TO ROCK

Dublin, 1992

He picked up the card and read through the verse for the third time. Over-sentimental as usual and inscribed in Brenda's cramped handwriting; *Happy Big Five- O – When are you coming over to see us again*? He fingered it for a moment then dropped it face down on the mantlepiece above the gas fire.

Fifty…I'm fifty.

Jeez.

That means by the law of averages I've lived over two-thirds of my life. He lowered himself into the old armchair, his eyes drifting round the room – the television, the occasional table with the scuffed legs, the new rug – the only thing less than fifteen years old in the flat – the faded carpet, the doors leading in turn into kitchen, bedroom, bathroom, the French window opening onto the tiny rectangle of verandah eight floors up, the only noise the hiss of the gas fire. It was quiet in the flat above. But it was early yet.

Fifty.

Jeez.

He glanced at the card again. At least she remembered.

He hadn't seen his sister since, when was it, seven years now when he'd finally scraped together the fare. He'd been there less than three days when he realised it was a mistake. The children, all boys, three of them, had sniggered at his accent, Brenda and Raymond having by now acquired a mid-Atlantic twang – necessary, they told him, to make themselves understood. He found this hard to accept. Toronto was full of Irish, for God's sake, Northern and Southern, he didn't see how it mattered. Oh, he was made welcome enough at first, but it was soon obvious to him that it was a duty invitation, a conscience thing. He'd overheard Raymond and Brenda arguing in low tones; "But he's my brother – he has nobody else," she'd pleaded. He'd cut the trip short, he couldn't even remember his excuse now, and flown home.

Fifty.

The hiss of the fire and the gentle heat sent him into a doze until the ring of the doorbell jerked him back to consciousness. The shouting was just starting in the flat above as it had done around this time every night for the past three weeks ever since they'd moved in.

He didn't get many visitors and he frowned as he pushed himself out of the chair, quickly checking round the room before crossing to the door.

Vic spread his arms wide and reached forward slapping him on the shoulders. "Hey! Hey!" he shouted; "How you doin', Frankie? – How you doin'?"

Frank stared at the man in front of him. Vic looked surprisingly little changed, his face a little lined, whose wasn't, a little jowled, that was all. The hair, suspiciously black, was still brushed low on his forehead, like his own had been then, like they all had been. Vic's eyes, too, seemed to throw out a glitter, a reflection from the light shining out from behind Frank.

"Well, aren't you gonna invite me in, Frankie-boy?"

Frank, unable to find the words, stepped aside and Vic sauntered past him and over towards the settee. "Well…Nice…Very nice, Frankie." He looked round the room.

What's nice about it, Frank thought. The woman above was screaming now at the man who retorted angrily when she paused for breath.

Vic moved over to the French window, leaned forward, looked out. "Great view."

Frank nodded. Ought to be a great view, eight floors up. And you had to like gasometers.

Vic turned back, spreading his arms again, palms out. "You're looking good, Frankie. How you been?"

"Okay – Yourself?"

"Great…Can't complain. Things are good…good." He nodded and beamed at Frank, dropped onto the settee, threw one flared trouser leg across the other and clasped his fingers, opened them, clasped them, still smiling, "Surprise, eh?"

"Yes…Quite a surprise."

"Thought it was time I looked you up. Took a while to find you but… Hey, here I am." He looked round the room again. "Uh…" He raised his eyebrows… "You married?"

Frank hesitated, shook his head. "Separated…nine years now." He heard something smash in the flat above. The man was shouting now – rough, vindictive.

"Oh… Sorry. Jeez, I'm sorry…What can I say? …It happens, y'know?" Vic hesitated, waggled his fingers, "Any…uh…?"

Frank shook his head. Vic nodded, shrugged. "Got two girls myself. Grown up now. One's a nurse, the other works in a bank – Doin' good, both of them."

"Nice," Frank said.

"Ever see any of the others?"

Frank shook his head. "No." There was something coming. Get to it, Vic. Get to the point.

"Ever play any now?"

"No." No. Not since…

"Still got it?"

Frank nodded, "Somewhere." He made a vague gesture.

"Ever think of having a go again?"

"What is this, Vic?"

"Hey, wait!...Wait! Take it easy, Frankie. I just thought you might like to…"

"Like to what?"

"Like to play again."

"Play again? You mean like…?"

Vic nodded, serious now. "Like before, yeah."

Frank started to laugh. He sat down on the arm of the chair. Like before. Like before Lukie. "You haven't changed, Vic."

83

Vic took it as a compliment. He grinned, shrugged his shoulders, spread his palms. He looked round the room. "I been thinking about it a while now, Frankie. This place – it's ready for us again. I can see it. We'd go down a bomb."

"We?"

"Yeah… You, me, Gerry, Tommy, Don, Mickey…All the guys. It'd be like it used be."

"No, Vic … Not like it used to be." Frank rose, walked to the window, looked out. "You seem to have forgotten something."

There was a moment of silence. "No, I haven't forgotten – But what's past is past, Frankie."

Frank looked across to where the gasometer loomed above the rooftops. He opened the window, stepped onto the narrow balcony. He leaned on the rail and glanced down. Far below a red Cavalier, two models out of date, was parked partly on the opposite kerb.

Vic was talking, talking fast now, talking eagerly; "I've seen the others. They're …keen…They say it depends…On you. They say if you agree they're ready… So… How about it, Frankie? What do you say?"

Frank looked over his shoulder. Vic was perched on the edge of the settee, half-turned towards him, eyes gleaming with excitement. Beyond him Frank could see the birthday card lying on the mantlepiece. A faint breeze tugged at his hair and he could smell the coming rain. He looked down at the street. A boy of about seven was skipping towards the Cavalier.

"I can see it, Frankie – Can't you? The old line up… Tommy on Bass, Don on drums, Gerry on the 'bone, Mickey on horn…You on sax…"

"What about lead?"

"Well, we haven't exactly got a lead yet. I thought we could maybe get by without…"

"You need lead guitar." Frank butted in. He looked down. The boy was climbing onto the bonnet of the Cavalier. "And while you're at it – get a sax player." He crossed his arms, hunched forward over the rail.

"Aw, come on, Frankie. We need you…We need *you*."

"Forget it." Frank leaned out. "That your car down there?"

"Red Cavalier? Yeah…Why?" The kid was standing on the roof now and two others were running across.

Frank shrugged. "Nothing."

"Look, Frankie." Pleading now. "I know how you feel about Lukie.

But that was… God, it must be over twenty-five years now."

Frank jerked round. "No! You haven't a clue how I feel! – You shouldn't have given him the keys!" He turned back into the room, walked quickly past Vic and into the bathroom. He leaned on the basin, staring into the mirror. The face looking back depressed him with its lines and grey stubble.

.….Lukie…Oh, Lukie. Lukie smiling, forever smiling. Baby-faced, curly-haired, blue-eyed, unpredictable Lukie, nineteen years old never had a music lesson in his life didn't know a treble clef from a semi-quaver playing lead guitar like a maestro. A natural. Everybody's kid brother… Everybody's responsibility. "Please look after him," his mother had pleaded. "He has to be watched all the time. He's a good boy but he's not…he's not quite……Please look after him."

And they had promised. Don't worry, they said, he'll be all right with us.

And Lukie one night, Saint Patrick's night, asking Vic for the keys, he needed a replacement string, walking out to the coach, getting in, starting the engine, God knows why, accelerating, accelerating down the hill towards the bay and through the barrier and off, straight off the quay into the water, dark water, nobody there to see… And when they winched him out the next morning they all stood there in a line watching, shivering, breath frosty in the cold air of the dawn, Lukie, arm reaching, still reaching out of the partly-open window for the help that wasn't there.

"You shouldn't have given him the keys!" he'd shouted at Vic. He'd picked up his saxophone case then and walked away…..

He twisted the tap, splashed some water onto his face, patted it dry, went back out to the living room. The woman in the flat above was sobbing now. He heard a smack, followed by a scream of pain. The ceiling shook as something thudded to the floor. He went across to the mantlepiece and picked up the card. "It's my birthday today – I'm fifty years old." He propped up the card on the mantlepiece. "I'm too old…too tired." He gave a bitter laugh. "Too tired to rock."

Vic leaned forward. "Aw, come on, Frankie. Age doesn't matter these days. Look at Dickie – still pulling them in… Joe, too."

"Dickie took a look into the future. He saw the end coming. He made the move at the right time."

Vic gave a dismissive wave. "So what, Frankie, what's a few years.

Jeez, I'm fifty-two myself in November. I can still belt them out – Listen." He jumped up and started to sing, gyrating his hips, one hand clasping an imaginary microphone, hoarse, off key. He stopped suddenly, flapped his hand. "Okay – a bit rusty maybe. But with practice, cutting down on the cigarettes, a little exercise…I'll be okay. I can do it…I can *do* it." He dropped back onto the settee, panting a little.

Frank crossed the room again to the balcony. There were four kids now – two on the bonnet, two on the roof. The rain was only minutes away. "You shouldn't have given him the keys."

"You don't forget easily, do you?" Vic, losing enthusiasm now, shifted uncomfortably on the settee.

"Why did you have to come here?" Frank turned, his back to the rail. "Why don't you just leave me alone and let me …let me enjoy my birthday. If it hadn't been for you Lukie would still be…" Jeez, he'd be forty-four.

Vic pushed himself up. "You trying to punish me, Frankie?"

"I didn't ask you to come here."

Vic faced him across the room. "You think I've forgotten about it? He was my responsibility, too. I loved him like a kid brother. You think I don't dream about it? You think I don't hurt? You got the monopoly on pain, Frank?" No Frankie now. His jaw quivered. "It's been with me all these years and I'm trying to…I'm looking for somebody…some one person… some one of the boys to say to me; 'It's okay, Vic – you weren't to know – It wasn't your fault'…I just want somebody to forgive me." He was staring at the floor. "I thought if I could get the band together again, then maybe…" He stopped and the room was silent save for the sobbing of the woman in the flat above.

Frank felt a twinge of pity for the man slowly disintegrating in front of him. "Okay," he said. "Maybe you're right – Maybe you just picked a bad day to call."

Vic sniffed, nodded. "I'm sorry I wasted your time. You're right. It was just a dream." He paused. "Anyway…the others – Mickey, Tommy…the others… they weren't really all that keen. They're all settled down now with tropical fish and wine-making kits and satellite dishes – Mickey's a granda, for God's sake." He looked away. "It's just… Time's going so quickly, y'know? I keep seeing this old guy in the mirror and I wanted to give it one more try – See if I could bring it all back." He turned towards the door. "But they were good times, Frank, you gotta admit that."

Frank nodded. "They were good times, Vic."

Vic reached for the door handle. "Sorry I intruded…Lousy life, isn't it, Frankie?" He stepped out. "Oh…" He raised his hand in a parting gesture. "Happy birthday."

Frank watched him walk to the staircase. When the top of Vic's head disappeared from view he stepped back in, closing the door. As he did so the gas fire gave a plop and the glow faded. He dug his hand into his pocket for a fifty-pence piece. He hadn't one. He went into the bedroom and sorted through the small change on the bedside cabinet. None there either.

He walked back into the living room. The French window was still open and the room was getting chilly. He went over and pulled the window shut, hesitated, opened it again, stepped over to the rail and looked down. The kids were scrambling off the Cavalier and running away. He watched Vic cross the street, unlock the door and lower himself stiffly inside. It started to rain then and the hiss of the sudden downpour muffled the sound of the starter. Frank watched the car bump off the kerb and chug up the street, slow at the junction and turn the corner.

"I forgive you," he said.

He sat with the case across his knees and listened to the rain slapping against the French window. He blew off the dust and the catches squeaked as he snapped them back. The saxophone was a little discoloured but not bad.

As he lifted it out something fluttered to the floor. He picked it up – an old promotional photograph. They were crowded together, holding their instruments, posing for the camera. He looked at the boy second left in the front row. "At least you'll never know what it's like to be fifty," he said.

He tried the keys. They were a little stiff, one or two completely seized up. He lifted the small bottle out of the case and shook it, opened it and oiled the linkage lightly, wiping off the surplus with his handkerchief, then worked the keys till they moved freely. The reed, when he picked it up, split between his fingers. He searched in the case again and found a sealed packet, opened it and examined the fresh reed. It looked okay. He moistened it with his tongue then gently inserted it into the mouthpiece, lifted the saxophone and blew a few experimental notes. It sounded not bad, not bad at all. He worked his lips around the mouthpiece, trying to get used to the feel again and went up and down the scale a few times. He began to play, slowly at first. After a minute he stood up, looped the strap over his head until the instrument hung comfortably then began to play faster, swaying now, foot tapping in time with the beat – *Roll over, Beethoven*...

There was a loud hammering above his head. He stopped playing and looked up. He went over to the table, pulled it across the carpet to the middle of the room until it was directly below the spot where the hammering had been and climbed up until his head was almost touching the ceiling. He raised the saxophone, arched his back and began to play;

Haaapppy Birthdaaay tooo youuu...Haaapppy Birthdaaay tooo youuu...Haaapppy Birthdaaay dear............

ACROSS THE WATER

Belfast, 1954

He sat by the window, pressed down on the pages of the textbook to stop them fanning over and tried to ignore the creaking of the floorboards above his head. He concentrated on the words in front of him. It was three months now and he was still having difficulty getting to grips with the strange language. His friend, Billy, had no trouble but then most subjects came easily to Billy.

He heard a bump from above and traced the footsteps across to where the big wardrobe stood. He forced his mind back to his homework. Verbs... conjugate the verbs; *je suis...tu es...il est...* A rattle of dishes came from the scullery. She had been in there a long time – longer than usual. He glanced sideways to where his father sat, offering his palms to the fire, rubbing them alternately against the backs of his hands, eyes searching for something in the flames.

The boy watched him carefully, not wishing their eyes to meet and ready to look away should his father turn towards him. *Mon pere est devant le feu,* he thought, then, suddenly pleased with himself, *et ma mere est dans la cuisine et ma frère –* no, I mean *non – mon frère est...mon frère est......My brother is upstairs getting ready because he is going away.*

He felt the ache coming back and looked across at the corner beside the gas meter where the toolbox sat, the padlock lying on top. He had tried to lift it once, the night his brother had brought it home. "That's the last one, Mammy," his brother had said, handing her the buff envelope. "I've been paid off." He had turned then and gone straight upstairs. He didn't come down for a long time. His mother had called him, told him his dinner was out. It was getting cold by the time he did come down and he only ate a few bites. He wasn't hungry, he'd said.

In the weeks since, he hadn't gone out much except for his Thursday night training and his match on Saturday. The boy had gone to see him once or twice and stood on the touchline with a dozen or so others, shouting encouragement, but it seemed his brother's heart was no longer in the game.

The boy wondered which suit he'd be wearing when he came downstairs. His brother was a snappy dresser. He had two suits and he looked a bit like Montgomery Clift when he was dressed up ready to go out.

His father lifted his cigarettes off the mantelpiece. He tore a strip from the margin of the newspaper, folded it, pushed an end into the flames and lit up, drawing deeply. He coughed once then settled down again, hunched forward, cigarette between forefinger and thumb. *Mon pere fumē la cigarette*…Is that right?

The room was quiet save for the tick of the clock and the occasional spit of the fire and the clink from the scullery. The boy didn't like this silence. The house was always full of noise – his mother chattering, his brother singing, wrestling with him on the faded carpet, pinning him down with strong hands, tickling him till he couldn't breathe, his mother shouting at his brother to stop he'll go into convulsions. His father was the quiet one. Like now.

He heard the feet cross to the landing, then the bump, bump on the stairs. His father threw his cigarette butt into the fire and sat up straight. The rattling in the scullery stopped.

His brother appeared, lugging the suitcase, tilted to negotiate the bend at the foot of the stairs. He was wearing his second best suit.

The boy had looked up Sunderland in his school atlas. It didn't look that far away. He couldn't understand why everyone had got so upset when his brother talked about it. It's just across the water, Mammy, his brother had tried to tell his mother. It's not as if I'm going to Canada like Joey. His friend, Joey, had been paid off the same day.

But she wasn't convinced. Maybe it was because his brother himself didn't want to go. I haven't any choice, he'd said. Well, I suppose I do have a choice – I can go to Sunderland or I can stand at the corner all day until it's time for tea.

His brother set the old suitcase beside the toolbox and laid his raincoat across it. He knelt, hinged back the toolbox lid, paused to light a cigarette, eyes narrowing as the smoke curled up, and began to check the contents. He had already checked them twice that day, the last time just before dinner.

Satisfied, he flipped down the lid, dropped the hasp and hooked the padlock in place, patted his pockets for the key, then clicked the padlock shut. He brushed his hand across the top where his initials were burnt into the wood. He looked at his wristwatch, threw a glance over at the clock, gave the watch a few winds then sat down in the chair at the other end of the table. No one had spoken.

"Here's a cup of tea." His mother came out of the scullery, carrying a mug and a plate of biscuits. "Do the rest of you want one?"

His father shook his head. The boy shook his and she disappeared into the scullery again.

His brother took a sip. He didn't touch the biscuits. He leaned forward and tossed his cigarette into the fire.

The boy tried again to concentrate on his homework: *Qu'est-ce que c'est? –* What is it?... *Quelle heure est il? –* What time is it? He looked at the clock...*Il est sept heure vingt-cinq.*

"What time will your boat get in?" His father. Trying.

"About six."

"You'd have been better with a berth."

"I'll be okay...sleep anywhere, you know me." His brother forced a grin.

It was quiet again.

After a while his brother looked at his watch. "Well...I suppose I'd better be on my way." He'd hardly touched his tea. He looked round the room, slapped his hands on the arms of the chair, sat up, hesitated, then pushed himself up and reached for his raincoat.

His mother came out of the scullery, wiping her hands on her apron and stood watching him.

He shrugged into the raincoat and turned to her. He tried to smile. "It won't be for long," he said. But there was no conviction. She reached up

91

quickly, pulled down his head and kissed his cheek. The boy looked away. His brother held her for a moment until she turned from him and went back into the scullery. The boy heard a sob as she closed the door.

His brother made to go after her but his father shook his head. "She'll be all right – it'll just take her a wee while to get used to it." He rose from the chair.

"Can I go with you to the bus stop?" the boy asked quickly. "I can help you carry your case."

"Okay…If you want."

The boy rushed to the bottom of the stairs where his navy burberry hung. He pulled it on.

"Ready?" his brother asked. The boy nodded and reached for the suitcase. He needed both hands to hold it clear of the floor.

His father held out his hand. His brother, awkward, shook it.

"Mind yourself now," The older man said. "Write us a wee letter and let us know how you're gettin' on." He opened the door and stood aside then followed them out.

It was cold. It had been raining and the footpath glistened in the light from the street lamps.

His brother cleared his throat. "Well…Cheerio, then."

"Cheerio," his father said and the two of them set off down the street. When they reached the lamp on the corner his brother turned. The boy looked back and could just make out the doorway where his father stood, hands in his pockets. His mother was there too, her hand at her mouth.

His brother waved once and his father raised his hand in response, then they were round the corner.

They trudged down the long dark street that led to the main road and the bus stop. The boy struggled with the suitcase. He was glad he hadn't picked the toolbox with its squat shape and narrow metal handle. As it was the suitcase banged against his leg and even with his two-handed grip he had to change sides every dozen or so steps.

"Here," his brother said. "I'll take that – It'll help to balance this." He nodded down at the toolbox.

"No…I'm okay…I can manage it all right."

His brother made to speak, then hesitated. "Okay." His voice sounded funny.

They passed the school, then the ropeworks. *J'ai froid...Il a froid...Elle a froid...*

"Did you ever do French?" the boy asked. Something to say. Normally he could have chatted away, easy in his brother's company. Tonight it seemed there was nothing to talk about.

"Me?...Naw...The three Rs was all we got...and a bit of geography. It's all different now."

"I hate French. It's not even the learnin' of the words... You have to speak it funny too – kind of through your nose."

"You stick with your French...and your other lessons too. Get yourself a clean job...wear a tie...not like me." His brother shortened his step so the boy could keep up with him.

What use is French? the boy thought. I want to be like you. I want to mend things...To have strong hands and thick wrists like yours. I want to smoke Blues and have two suits and a toolbox with my initials burnt into the lid. I want...

It started to rain again. It was a good six or seven minutes to the main road and there was no more talk between them as they walked as quickly as the boy could manage.

As they turned the corner a bus was just leaving the stop. "You've missed it," the boy said. Glad.

"There'll be another along in a minute or two," his brother said.

The traffic swished past. A man was sitting astride a bike, unfolding an oilskin cape. Across the road a group of men huddled around the window of the electrical shop. Beyond them the boy could see the television's black and white flicker.

"Do you think we'll ever have one of those?" he asked as they stepped into the biscuit factory doorway.

"Aye, probably...when things get better again," his brother replied.

"They cost seventy pounds. Jackie Quinn's da's gettin' one on Saturday." He watched the cyclist pull the cape over his shoulders then push away from the kerb. *La bicyclette.*

A fat woman with an umbrella joined them in the doorway.

"Have you cleaned my boots yet?" his brother asked. His football boots. The boy got a half-crown every week for cleaning them.

"Not yet – I'm waitin' for the dirt to harden then I can brush it off easier."

"Don't forget to put plenty of Dubbin on...Mind you don't put it on the toecaps."

"I know – you tell me that every week."

"Here's one now," the fat woman said, starting to wrestle down her umbrella.

The boy's heart started to race; *I have to tell him...I have to let him know.*

The trolley wires started to zing. They swung and glinted in the lamplight. His brother picked up his toolbox and moved across the footpath. The boy followed with the case. He could see the lights of the bus a hundred or so yards away.

"Here...take this." His brother handed him a coin – a half-crown. "For cleanin' my boots. I'll send you some more in a week or two."

Tell him now. Hurry up...There isn't much time.

A cheer erupted from the crowd of men across the road. His mouth was dry. *Tell him.*

The bus was coming up fast. A man was leaning out from the platform, swinging from the bar. The boy's heart was thumping now. *Say it.*

The man jumped off the bus at a run, slowing down as he passed them, a young man, long hair, long jacket, velvet collar, tight trousers. He thrust his hands into his pockets, his shoes squelching as he strutted past.

The bus shuddered to a halt and the fat woman, breathing loudly, heaved herself on board.

His brother set the suitcase on the platform. The conductor slid it into the luggage space below the stairs.

"Well...I'll be seein' you, then." His brother held out his hand. The boy gripped it tight. *Now...Tell him...Tell him.*

"Cheerio," he said. He still held onto his brother's hand.

"Are ye gettin' on or not?" the conductor shouted.

His brother gently extricated his hand and stepped backwards onto the platform, the toolbox by his side.

The conductor rang the bell.

Now. He opened his mouth to speak, hesitated, then; *"Je t'aime,"* he said.

His brother leaned forward. "What?...What was that?" And the bus started to pull away, picking up speed. His brother stood on the platform, feet braced, holding the bar with one hand, the toolbox in the other.

They watched each other until the bus reached the bend in the road and disappeared out of sight.

The crowd outside the electrical shop began to disperse.

"Au revoir," he whispered.

He didn't like the long dark street. The lamps were spaced too far apart. He was afraid of the even darker gateways of the ropeworks on either side and the rustling noises from the depths of the entries.

He always ran down the street. On the darkest night with fear at his shoulders he could run from one end to the other in a little under a minute and a half, passing the street lamps, racing his shadows, never winning as they stretched forward and disappeared, to be replaced by others, overtaking, surging ahead.

Tonight, head hunched over, hands sore, blistered, deep in the pockets of his burberry, no longer afraid, he walked slowly in the knowledge that the closer he got to home, the further away his brother would be.

MARLON

Belfast, 1988

I'd seen him once or twice in the years between. Surprisingly few times when you consider we couldn't have been all that far away from each other – me moving back near the old neighbourhood, him probably not moving at all from wherever it was he used to live in those days – we never did find out for sure.

The first time we were crossing North Road bridge. He was walking towards us, hunched over the way I remembered him, battling the wind gusting across the parapet.

"There's Marlon!" I said.

"Who?" Annie, beside me. Annie always beside me.

"Marlon...Back there! We just passed him!...There! – With the dog!" He came into view in the mirror, the brown and white mongrel trotting in front, straining against the leash.

"And who is Marlon?" asked Annie.

"He used to hang around the wall when I was a kid."

"The wall?"

"There was this gable wall. At the top of our street. He must be sixty if he's a day but he still looks the same."

"Marlon...Marlon...Now there's a name." Annie's into names – traditional, trendy, variations, origins. Give her a name and she'll tell you all you want – and sometimes don't want – to know.

"We called him that because he mumbled all the time…Like Brando? We never knew his real name." I smiled to myself… Memories……

……I'd been on my way to Mr Porter's shop, skirting round the puddles, anxious to get back before the rain came on again. It was getting dark as I ran round the corner and straight into him. He grunted, grabbed me as I started to fall and just as quickly let go. I backed away and at that moment the streetlights came on. He was around mid-height, wearing an old donkey jacket, collar raised, head tucked in, long beaky nose, black hair, rain-soaked, growing down on his forehead in a v.

"Sorry, mister," I said. But it was like he'd forgotten me already. He was looking at the wall.

It was the gable end of the next row of houses up from ours. Over the years it had got covered with layers of drawings and messages. We didn't call it graffiti then. Genuine brush-painting – none of your hurried, fuzzy-edged spray-can jobs. They took pride in their work in those days.

He stood there a moment then walked over and turned and leaned his back against the wall like he was trying it out. He slid his hands into his pockets, seeming to blend into the lines and shapes and patterns on the plastered surface, and faced down towards the twin rows of tight-fitted houses that was our street. I don't think he noticed me walk away.

And that was the beginning. Each night he would take up position when the echoes of Robertson's factory horn had faded and the workers had all gone. He would stand there till bedtime, shoulders hunched, hands in pockets, watching down the street like he was waiting for something.

Nobody knew where he had come from, where exactly he lived, although it must have been somewhere close by. Some of us tried to get him into conversation but all we got in return was a mumble of half-spoken words.

It wasn't that long, however, until we discovered that Marlon, now a constant in our lives, was an accomplished beggar. One night I was walking home from the pictures with my brother, eight years older than me and just finished his apprenticeship. Marlon, must, in some way, have got wind of this. When we reached the corner he was there as he always was and we spoke to him as we always did. As we went past he said to my brother – in a clear voice, I noticed – "Would you have any odds on you?"

I didn't know what he meant by this, but my brother did. He reached into his pocket and handed Marlon a couple of bob. He seemed pleased at having been asked. When I look back, I suppose it was the first acknowledgment he was now a proper working-man......

It was a late September evening when I set off down the main road.
"Twenty-five minutes," he'd said. "– Four times a week."
"Twenty-five minutes? Why not the even half-hour?" I buttoned my shirt.
He shrugged, removed the stethoscope. "I'm only a doctor – What do I know? ... Probably some government-funded study and they've concluded a twenty-five minute walk three times a week is the key to immortality. Next thing they'll be advising us to give up smoking and eat five pieces of fruit a day. It's up to you. I can give you pills – slow you down. Is that what you want?"
"No – No pills."
I should have heeded Annie earlier. "See the doctor," she'd pleaded. "You can't go on like this."
Deadlines. Long hours. More deadlines. More long hours. Unable to sleep. The constant fatigue. I'm okay, I said. I can handle it...
Until the night I was driving home along a route I'd travelled a thousand times and suddenly not knowing if I needed to turn right or turn left, the traffic building up while I tried to think and the horn from the car behind.
I got out, walked back and he wound down the window – big guy, blond hair, red face, tight collar, testosterone-super-plus. I reached in, pulled out the keys, fluffy dice and all, and lobbed them over a hedge into a garden. His mouth was still open as I got back into my car, opted for the left turn and had to detour back, getting home twenty minutes late.
The doctor had leaned forward, serious now. "Take the advice, Tony. Exercise works – it really does work."
I put it off – always found some excuse. Until the night Annie said she needed some cash for the morning. She runs a little second-hand-bookshop-cum-coffee-shop and doing all right. I picked up the car keys. Put them down again.
So there I was – twenty-five minutes, four times a week, the secret of perfect health – walking down the road, arms swinging, a little out of breath the way it was meant to be. I reckoned: do the walk, get the money, back home, cup of tea, News At Ten, that wasn't so hard, was it?

I walked briskly, getting to enjoy it after a while. The moon was bright, disappearing now and then behind the clouds.

I was almost at the bank when I spotted him ahead of me, the dog trotting alongside. He was a little slower than the last time I'd seen him and I was quickly catching up. I stopped at the cash machine and kept an eye on him as I keyed in my number. He turned the corner where Prestons used to be. I collected the card and the money and hurried after him.

I caught up, drew alongside. "Marlon?" He was breathing hard, the dog straining at the leash.

He didn't even look round. "Hello, Tony."

Now you've got to remember we hadn't seen each other for the best part of thirty years and I wasn't exactly in the first flush of youth anymore. My first feeling was of gratitude – maybe I didn't look so bad after all. "How are you, Marlon?" I asked.

Was there a slight hesitation? "Okay," he replied. He walked on, the dog padding in front like it was on a mission.

"Which way are you going?"

He nodded across the street in the direction of the shopping centre. They were building an extension, had knocked down a whole row of houses to make a car park. A chain-link fence closed it off. It was hard to remember the geography of things.

My intention had been to go straight up the street and circle back home. I'd worked out it would take me the full twenty-five minutes. Instead; "I was just going that way myself." I said.

Marlon nodded, mumbled something and we crossed the street. We walked in silence for a minute then it just came out, don't ask me why; "I have to walk for twenty-five minutes, four times a week – doctor's orders." I immediately felt a little foolish but he gave no indication he'd even heard me. The dog stopped, sniffed the fence, lifted its hind leg then trotted on.

We reached the end of the fence and I was confronted by a plywood hoarding, seven feet high. It hadn't been there before but then neither had the shopping centre if you thought back far enough. I stopped dead. "What happened?" I asked. "There used to be a street here...and a school... and Mrs Martin's shop and..." I looked around me. What had once been Robertson's factory was now an enterprise park according to the sign on the gate. "Used to be ...houses..."

Marlon spoke; "There are still houses…you just can't see them from here." He walked, a little painfully now I thought, along the side of the plywood hoarding to the end and I followed, almost falling over an iron bollard at the opening.

There were houses, sure enough – two dozen or so – new, brown rustic-brick semis, a flagged area at the side of each. There used to be three times that many houses in the same space. There was a notice on the side wall of the nearest house – *No Ball Games.* I tried to figure out where our house had been but it was no use. I dropped my head. Looked away.

The wall was still there but the graffiti was different. Where it once said *SHUEY LOVES PATSY* and *UP THE GLENS* someone had started a mural and abandoned it half-way. Across the coloured backdrop was scrawled *S S RUC* and *REMBER 1690.* Beyond it the few original houses were boarded up shells, grass and weeds where the bricks met the footpath. A yellow bulldozer was quarantined behind another wire fence.

Marlon walked over to the wall, turned and leaned against it. The dog flopped down with a sigh. I went over and stood beside him and leaned back. It felt strangely comforting. Marlon was gazing straight ahead, seeing things and I wished I could see them too.

He spoke; "Twenty-five minutes?" Then; "Why not the even half-hour?"

Precisely, I thought. I shrugged.

"Some doctor," he mumbled.

All the new houses had satellite dishes, facing south. When I'd lived there we had an old black and white Philips with a fourteen-inch screen, took three minutes for the picture to come up, Daleks could only move on metal, William Hartnell forgot his lines and the scenery swayed.

"I'm going away," said Marlon.

"Oh?… Where?"

"I've got a sister – down near Enniskillen. She wants me to go and live with her. It's out in the country…fields and trees and things…good for the oul lungs, she says. She's been at me a while now. Only, the thing is… she's got two cats." He was looking down at the dog now and, sensing something, it lifted its head. In the light from the street lamp I saw one ear was missing like it had been chewed off.

I was already working it out: four times twenty-five – that's almost the same as seven-times fifteen. The dog was lying motionless, head between his paws. "I could look after him …if you want me to, that is."

He was still staring into space. "It's not the same any more…Used to be they'd speak to you…pass the time of day. Now they drop their eyes and walk near onto the road to get past you."

"You've been coming here all these years?"

"Except the time I had a wisdom tooth pulled out." He nodded over at the new houses. "The people who used to live here…they're gone… all of them… dead or in Ballybeen." He reached me the end of the leash. "He doesn't have a name. I never could think of one…" He frowned; "You've no cats, have you?…He doesn't like cats."

I shook my head, "No…no cats."

"He's a good old boy…no trouble. Feed him once a day – nothing fancy. Leftovers is what he's used to."

"How much do you want for him?" I reached into my pocket for the money I'd just drawn out.

He shook his head. "Just give him a good home." He turned away then and I knew it was time for me to go. I wasn't sure what to do next and I tried clicking my tongue but it came out like a bad impression of Donald Duck. The dog rose and shook itself. I flipped the leash. The dog looked at me then looked at Marlon.

"Go on," he said and waved it away. The dog lowered its head and I turned to leave. "Wait," Marlon said.

I stopped, thinking he'd already changed his mind.

"Would you have any odds on you?"

I smiled and dug out all the loose change I had and gave it to him. He didn't say anything, just turned and looked down a street that was no longer there.

I walked away, the dog trotting beside me. I wondered what Annie would say – I'd only come out to get some money from the cash point.

As we passed the compound with the yellow bulldozer, a feeling of resentment started to grow in me. The dog pulled sideways, sniffed, then lifted his leg against the wire. I resisted the temptation to join him. He shook himself, his good ear flapping, and looked up at me. I stooped and patted him on the head. "Attaboy," I said.

I looked back towards the corner. An elbow projected out from the end of the wall. I called out; "What's your name?…Your real name."

There was a pause, then; "John," he said.

The moon passed behind a cloud. "It's a fine name." The night air was still, crisp, distant sounds of traffic.

"Goodbye, John," I said.

I never saw him again. I walked round that way a week or so later and they'd knocked down the wall and the remaining houses. They'd put up a site hut and yet another fence and the foundations were already dug.

I try to imagine him down there in the country but the picture won't come. He belongs to the streets and the shadows and I can't see him in open spaces. But he often comes into my mind and I hope he's content there living with his sister and the cats and that the people accept him for what he is. May their pockets always be full of loose change.

The dog? The dog has settled in well. We call him Vincent – Annie's idea soon as she saw him.

I can't say I'm sleeping any better and I still feel tired all the time. I take Vincent out every night around half-past ten. I take him out for fifteen minutes. He pees a lot. I have to get out of bed and let him into the garden around half-three in the morning and again at seven.

But you know what they say: As long as you have your health........

EXITS AND ENTRANCES

Belfast, 1968

In the autumn of 1968 when he was a few days short of his twenty-third birthday my younger brother went for a high ball in a penalty-area scramble in the closing minutes of an early-season game. He nodded the ball towards the goalmouth and on his way down collided heads with the opposing centre-half. The centre-half walked round in circles, hunched over, shouting expletives, holding his head. My brother lay where he had fallen.

He was unconscious when they slid him into the back of the ambulance and he was still unconscious when they wheeled him into Emergency. By the time I got there he was already in theatre, my parents and sister sitting in a row on the plastic waiting-room chairs.

When the surgeon came out he told us he had removed the blood clot pressing on my brother's brain but it was too early to make a prognosis. He was now deep in coma and all we could do was wait and, if we thought it might help, pray.

"Coma? For how long? How bad is it?"

The surgeon shook his head. "Days...months... Maybe..." He didn't finish. He didn't need to.

"Can we see him?" asked my sister, ever in control. Typical big sister. She would comfort me, say all the things I wanted to hear when I was a kid and scared of just about everything. But even she couldn't make a difference this time.

Ben lay there, head covered in bandages, dark bruises round his eyes, linked by tubes and wires to the machines beside the bed, the only movement the steady rise and fall of his chest...

The next week saw no change. We fell into a pattern – my parents doing the days, Pamela and I taking turns with the nights. I slept when I got the chance. Talk to him, the doctors said... Keep talking to him. We can't be sure, of course, but he may hear you. Talk about anything – anything at all.

And that's what we did.

Now, here's where I have to say that talking to my brother was not something I was in the habit of doing. The fact is he and I just didn't get along. We had been close enough when we were younger, but by the time we were in our teens it seemed the only thing we had in common was a surname. The older by two years, I studied hard at school, determined to get on in life – escape my working-class background. Ben, on the other hand, couldn't wait to leave school and made no effort, to my parents' dismay, to follow any sort of career path, taking, instead, any odd job that came along. And thus we grew apart. In time I moved into my own flat and we only saw one another at the occasional family gathering.

Now area rep for an office equipment company, I called each month with my customers. I shook their hands, gave them a warm, practised smile, made sure of eye contact. I enquired after their children whose names were stored in my notebook. I told them the latest rehearsed joke, persuaded them to take advantage of that week's special offer on carbon paper, took their orders and demonstrated the latest office gadget to make their businesses run more efficiently. Gadgets like the DX7.

The most recent in a line of hand-held dictating machines, the DX7 was a long way from the old mains-powered recorder taking up valuable desk space. Brad The Impaler had given me my sales target. That month I was targeted to sell fifty. Now, halfway through the month I'd taken orders for six. The reason for this was simple – the DX7 was a piece of crap.

Aside from a tendency for the tape to jam, the design was poor and I'd told Brad so. Timidly, I'd raised it with him: "It's all right, Mr Lewis, for a right-handed person where the relative positions of the speaker mouthpiece and the control buttons are okay but if you're left-handed this can be awkward. This is putting off a lot of my customers."

But Brad Lewis didn't want to know. I suspect he had imported a crate load of the DX7s and needed to offload them. "Tell them to turn it the other way round ...or use their right hand like normal people."

Now, if you are a left-handed person it's the natural inclination to want to use that hand, right? – Turning the DX7 the other way put the speaker mouthpiece in the wrong position. But this was Brad The Impaler. Since taking over the company he had become even more obnoxious and had already that year demoted Harry Vine and Alan Harris and sacked three other reps. His was a rule of fear.

They say we should talk to you, Ben ...keep talking to you... Ironic, isn't it, since we've hardly spoken a word to each other in, what, six, seven years?... Anyway, that's what they say.... So, what'll I talk about? The weather? What I've done with myself today? What you've done with yourself today?... Sorry, I shouldn't have said that... I'm sorry... Can you hear me, Ben?... I'm sorry... It's just... It's just I'm finding this a bit awkward. They say you may be able to hear me... but then again...... Anyhow, you know what?... I can't think of a thing to say. Not a thing!... Some salesman.....

It was towards the middle of the second week they brought him in. I'd got held up by protestors blocking the road and by the time I arrived at the hospital my sister had already left. My brother was alone in a side ward, separated from the main ward by a windowed partition. The old man was on the opposite side close to the ward entrance and I didn't notice him at first. But he shouted something as I went past and I glanced over. He was propped up by pillows, one frail arm waving. A nurse went across and spoke to him, seemed to calm him down and I went on in to Ben. There was still no change, except for his stubble. His birthday had come and gone a couple of days earlier and there were cards on the bedside cabinet.

I unzipped my briefcase and tried to catch up on some work. Brad had been hounding me – memos, phone messages, wanting to know how the sales of the DX7 were going. The fact was they weren't going well at all. My six sales had increased to nine and the month end was seven days away.

Across the main ward the old man was shouting again. Something about the cost of princes. I opened my sales folder and wondered what I was going to do.

Representative, Ben...Now there's a word. Sounds good, doesn't it? That's what we call ourselves these days...But we're salesmen...We sell things, nothing more. Some people sell milk, some sell hats, some women sell their bodies, for God's sake... Me? I sell paper and pens and cardboard folders and notebooks and calendars... There's this thing, this hand-held dictating machine – the DX7. The greatest thing since the wheel, Brad says – he's my boss – Brad The Impaler we call him. He's on my back wanting me to sell fifty of these things this month – fifty! You know how many I've sold so far? – nine!...That's right – nine! You see, there's this problem...Well, it's not a problem if you're right-handed...But if you're left-handed you have to... ...

On the way out the next morning as I passed the old man I noticed there was a blank space where the name should be on the clipboard hanging at the foot of his bed. A young nurse, I hadn't seen her before, was coming down the ward. She smiled at me, leaned over and took the old man's hand, held his wrist and checked his pulse.

"Who is he?" I asked.

"We don't know who he is… They found him in Bedford Street…lying round the side of the Group Theatre. We don't know if he has family or anything – We don't know who to contact."

"What's the matter with him?"

She hesitated. "I don't know if I should be saying… Och, I suppose it does no harm. He's had a stroke and there are other things as well. His heart's very weak…" She lowered her voice. "To tell you the truth he's very far through. We're doing all we can but…" She stopped. Her eyes said the rest.

"He reminds me of somebody," I said.

She nodded. "We've all known someone like him." She tucked the bedclothes round him, gave me a sad smile and walked away.

I stood over the old man for a moment. Suddenly he spoke; "Pipes and whistles…Pipes and whistles." He waved an arm and his eyes opened but he stared straight in front of him. Then his head dropped back and his eyes closed again. I turned quietly and went out of the ward.

I'm worried, Ben – scared, if you really want to know. I'm going to lose my job – I know it. I haven't got any more orders for the DX7 and tomorrow's the end of the month. I've been getting these urgent messages from Brad – you don't know what he's like – telling me to ring him and I haven't because I'm afraid... What do I do, Ben? If only I could be like you... like you were – you know – taking everything in your stride. Even when we were kids you never worried about anything, you were never afraid of anything... And there was I – older, bigger – scared of just about everything. So stupid, really, when you think about it – scared of dogs, of falling off my bike... scared of the dark. Hallowe'en stories, remember those? – they were the worst...stories about goblins and ghosts and banshees and...

And the Dark Angel.

When we were kids we went once to a Saturday matinee to see *The Leprechaun King* – a piece of Irish whimsy, all little men in green tights and pointy hats, obligatory pretty Irish colleen, handsome young newcomer – and Dilly, an old rascal with a thick mop of grey hair and a hooked nose and a tendency to poach on the rich landowner's property. I was enjoying it until fifteen minutes from the end when Dilly took sick after falling into the river. He lay in bed, gravely ill, his mongrel dog, Finbar, on the floor beside him. Outside the cottage the wind began to howl and the music, foreboding, started to swell and then out on the road, coming towards the cottage, appeared a tall, thin figure in a long grey hooded gown and carrying a scythe. The hood was open at the front but the thing was there was no face. As it drew closer the music got louder, scarier. There had been earlier talk about The Dark Angel of Death and we all knew that this was he.

The Dark Angel strode up to the door and pushed it open, but he hadn't reckoned on Finbar... Cut to the cottage interior and The Dark Angel entering the room and moving slowly towards the bed. Cut to Finbar rising on his haunches, teeth bared. Cut to The Dark Angel leaning over Dilly. Cut to Finbar, snarling, launching himself at The Dark Angel. Cut to the exterior and The Dark Angel retreating down the road, waving the scythe in fury. Cut to the interior again and Dilly making a miraculous recovery – all of this to the cheers of the kids in the cinema...

...Cut to the emergency exit and me reaching for the panic bar.....

The hair was white now, longer, sparser, the face thinner. His name was Ronan Cassidy, a well-known character actor of that time along with Joe Tomelty, J. G. Devlin, Harold Goldblatt... But whereas the others continued to dominate the local theatre, Ronan Cassidy, suddenly and inexplicably, dropped out of sight. Inevitably there were stories, all kinds of rumours, all of them different, but after *The Leprechaun King* no one seemed to know what happened to him and after a few years had gone by no one talked about him any more.

Looking back, I don't know why I didn't tell the nurses.

I had a nephew, Pamela's little boy, six years old. Any time I asked him why he always blew bubbles through his straw or splashed in the puddles in his new shoes or rode his go-cart into the table leg, his answer was; "Because". And I suppose that's as good an answer as any when you're six. And maybe that's what I wanted to be on that autumn night – six years old and not having to justify everything I did – or didn't – do.

Because.

The ward was quiet. I glanced at my watch. It was almost two a.m. My briefcase sat at my feet, I had papers on my knees trying to reconcile the other sales' totals for the month. They, too, had suffered. In truth, I had been stopping early for the past three or so weeks, trying to slip in a few hours sleep when I could, but my sales were badly down, on top of the problem with the DX7. I knew I was in big trouble with Brad Lewis for not contacting him. I glanced down at the sample DX7 peeking from my briefcase and picked it up, looked at it, turned it over, examined the other side, fiddled with the buttons. Set it back and turned my chair sideways a little, stretched out my legs, closed my eyes.

I must have dozed off for a few minutes. I jerked awake, yawned, stretched my arms wide and was suddenly conscious of being watched. I turned my head and my brother was lying there looking at me. We stayed that way a full thirty seconds and then his mouth moved. He was trying to say something but only a faint sound came out. I got up and leaned over him. He ran his tongue over his lips and tried again. His voice, weak from almost a month's lack of use, was little more than a whisper; "Did we win?"

I put the payphone back on the cradle and wiped my eyes and went back to the ward. They were carrying out tests on Ben so I picked up my briefcase and went along the corridor to the waiting room. The curtains round Ronan Cassidy's bed were closed as I passed. He mumbled something in his sleep.

The waiting room was empty. I opened my briefcase and brought out the DX7.

"Message for Brad Lewis:

Dear Mr Lewis. Apologies for not responding to your messages but I have been struggling to find a way to overcome the problems with the position of the buttons on the DX7 and I think I have come up with a solution. I can't believe, in the end, how simple it is. My suggestion is this: Pick up the DX7 with the left hand so that the thumb rests comfortably on the record button. Wrap the fingers of the same hand round the casing as far as they will go, making sure you maintain a firm grip, until the third finger touches the tape advance button, apply pressure on the record button and shove the DX7 up your arse.

Yours sincerely,

Edwin J Cairns.

PS – If there is any room left do the same with your job."

I stood at the post box for a moment, the package in my hand, then dropped it through the opening and skipped back over the road to the hospital like I had wings on my ankles. Dawn was still a couple of hours away, the road clear of traffic.

When I got back to the ward the doctors had gone and my brother was sleeping again but this time it was a different kind of sleep. I went across to Ronan Cassidy's bed and looked in. He, too, was sleeping peacefully, cawing noises coming from his open mouth. I slid my hand between the curtain and the end of the bed, at the same time reaching into my pocket for a pen.

I was still standing there when the young nurse appeared. I hadn't heard her approach. A moment earlier and she would have caught me. But the clipboard was back in its place.

She checked his pulse, touched his brow. "Poor old man. He has nobody…He's all alone and he'll die all alone."

Across the ward and through the doorway opposite I could see my brother. He was still sleeping. My mother and father and sister were on their way and would be there soon. "No," I said. "…He won't." I sat down on the chair and pulled it closer to the bed and we waited together for that old angel with the scythe. It was the autumn of 1968 and none of us knew what was coming our way but in that early morning in the silence of that hospital ward I wasn't scared. I wasn't scared at all.

Towards dawn he stirred in his sleep, talking sporadically, mostly ramblings that I couldn't understand. In the distance I could hear the noise of traffic starting to build, the beginning of another day. On the far side of the ward, through the partition window I could see my mother and father and sister with my brother. He was awake again, sitting up, sipping some water. He looked over at me and slowly rotated his wrist and raised his thumb. I did the same back to him.

I was out of a job but I felt sure something would turn up. What it would be I had no idea. I felt a sudden urge to laugh – I imagined sitting in front of an interview panel and someone would ask; "And tell us, Mr Cairns – Why did you leave your last job?"

And I would reply; "Because."

Ronan Cassidy turned his head towards me. "Sans everything," he said. He held out his hand, reaching for something. His eyes were open but he was looking far beyond me. "Is that you, J.G.?…Are you there?" He seemed afraid.

Through the window I could see the first faint streaks of light appear in the sky. I leaned across, took his hand, held on. It was bony, dry and it trembled a little.

"Yes," I said…"I'm here."

BUDGERIGARS

Belfast, 1957

Kenny was smiling, a big wide smile, wider than I've ever seen.

Kenny's three years older than me and although I say it myself, I know he's my brother and all, I think he's very handsome. He's got this black curly hair and smooth skin and the whitest of teeth. He's so handsome. Especially when he smiles.

My father had just lifted the budgerigar out of the shoebox and set it into the big cage, the one we used to keep the pigeons in. It was all of nine inches from the top of its head to the tip of its tail feathers. It was blue, a deep, deep blue and it hopped onto the perch and started to bob its head up and down like it was agreeing with us about something.

And that's why Kenny was smiling.

"What'll we call him?" asked my father. He filled the little hopper with seed and hooked it onto the side of the wire, closed the door and turned the little catch.

I had the name without even thinking about it. "Big Blue," I said. "We'll call him Big Blue."

"Big Boo!" shouted Kenny and clapped his hands. "Big Boo!"

And we all laughed.

It was another of my father's notions. I remember him hammering and sawing out in the back shed until the cage – we called it a coop then – was built. It was six feet square and sat up on four wooden legs. "Pigeons like to be high," he said.

I didn't much like the pigeons – smelly, noisy, coo-cooing all day and half the night so I wasn't sorry when my father got rid of them.

Then there was Sam.

Sam was a mongrel. "Pure-bred mongrel," my father said when he brought him home, a piece of string looped through his collar. My mother rolled her eyes at me, the way she does when my father takes one of his notions.

He hammered and sawed until he'd made the kennel – a proper, sturdy kennel made of eight-ply with a sloping felt roof.

He was a good carpenter, my father, and I suppose working for a builder meant there was no shortage of off-cuts, although now and then I got the feeling that an eight by four sheet would suddenly become a six by three.

I remember him making these little plywood Irish cottages one year coming up to Christmas. He made dozens of them. Every night he would bring home a bundle of off-cuts, saw them to size, nail them together and stick on little block chimneys before painting on doors and windows and curtains and gluing tiny strips of straw onto the roofs. He was going to sell them, make a few bob for Christmas, get my mother the fur boots she'd always wanted.

Christmas came and went that year. He sold half a dozen or so and the rest sat in rows under the bed until mid-February and a cold snap came along and he burnt them one night when we ran out of coal. My mother never did get her fur boots.

He took Sam for a walk one night, the first time he'd ever taken him out. He'd been watching the clock and around a quarter to eight he stood up. "Think I'll take the dog for a walk," he said, lifting the leash from the hook inside the cupboard door. "Come on, boy."

He came back alone. "Damn dog," he said. "Took him off the lead and he ran off. Wouldn't come back when I called. I searched all round the roads but couldn't find him anywhere. Damn dog." He looked over at me. "Don't worry – we'll get another one." But we never did and it was a long time before I saw Kenny smile again.

I'm not sure what happened when Kenny was being born. I overhear bits of conversation now and again. I hear things like "too long in the birth canal", whatever that means, and them having to use forceps but that's all I know and I don't really understand. He's my brother and that's the only thing matters far as I'm concerned.

It wasn't long before we had about a dozen budgies. The most common colour is green and we had a few of those. We had yellow ones as well and even some with yellow bodies and green wings but none of them looked as good as Big Blue.

He wasn't a young bird, Big Blue. I reckon he had been badly treated at some time because he could be vicious, nipping anyone who tried to stroke him. Except for Kenny who could put his whole hand into the cage and Big Blue would nuzzle his head against his finger.

To give the birds more flying space my father sometimes let them out into the main shed where he'd hung some perches from the roof. This was the time Kenny loved. He would sit out in the shed with the budgies fluttering round his head. He would hold out his hand and call, "Big Boo!" and Big Blue would swoop down and perch on his outstretched finger.

And Kenny would smile.

"Soon be breeding season," my father announced one night as we sat down for our dinner. Kenny was frowning and curling up his lip as he gripped his spoon. He eats everything with a spoon. He holds it tight in his fist and scoops up the food my mother cuts into little pieces for him.

"Eat your greens, Kenny," ordered my father.

Now, here's the problem; Kenny doesn't like vegetables. If it was up to me I wouldn't give him any in the first place, avoid the hassle, y' know? I put this theory to my father once. "He has to eat his greens – they're good for him," he replied and that was that. You don't argue with my father.

My mother is long-suffering. She needs to be, married to my father. She would tend to be like me and not push the vegetables bit. But my father has a thing about "good wholesome food."

I remember once he was going on at Kenny about his greens. "Eat them up, Kenny, or you'll never be able to…" And he stopped at that because he knew, like I knew, like my mother knew and, God knows, maybe even Kenny knew, that all the vegetables in the world would never make him able to do anything. He went to the special care school and they were patient with him and tried to teach him things and they praised him and made him happy but, at the end of it all, eating and going to the toilet and sleeping and smiling was all Kenny would ever do.

Breeding season came around and my father had everything ready. He had made half a dozen breeding cages each with a hole bored in one side. To the outside of each cage he hooked on a little nesting box also with a hole in the side so that the holes matched up and the birds could go from one to the other. Each nesting box had a trapdoor lid and a floor that slid out like a tray. The middle of the floor was carved in the shape of a saucer. "To hold the eggs," he said. I didn't know it then but I was about to have my first sex lesson.

My father paired off the birds and the mating began. I thought at first they were fighting and shouted at my father to stop them but he just laughed. "Everything's the way it's meant to be," he said.

One night, a few weeks later, he called to me. When I went out to the shed he beckoned me over to one of the nest boxes. The hen was out in the breeding cage watching us, head tilted to the side. My father hinged up the trapdoor lid. I had to stand on his toolbox to see in and there, lying on the carved out floor of the box was a tiny egg. He gently lowered the lid and the hen hopped back across the breeding cage and disappeared through the hole into the nest box.

That was the beginning. Over the next two or three weeks several eggs appeared – as much as four in each nest box. By now each hen was spending most of the time inside the nest box, each cock keeping watch near the hole.

Then one night as I was cleaning my shoes at the kitchen step I heard it. At first I thought it was the squeak of Kenny's wheelchair back in the living room. Then I heard it again – the faintest of cheeps coming from one of the cages.

My father was out somewhere and, full of curiosity, I dragged over the toolbox, stepped up and raised the trapdoor lid. There were two of them – tiny pink, fleshy, eyeless creatures, little bigger than a thumbnail, feebly moving little stumps of limbs. The hen was out in the cage kicking up a row so I carefully lowered the lid and went into the house to tell Kenny.

It wasn't long after that when the rest hatched out and we had over twice as many birds as we had started with.

The chicks were about three weeks old and it was getting near nightfall. My father was checking the nest boxes. Most of the trays slid out easily but one tended to stick a little. As he tugged, it suddenly came free and although he tried to catch them the chicks, four of them, rolled over the edge and fell to the floor of the shed. I watched in horror as they struggled, waving their tiny stumps of wings and I knew they were badly injured. I looked up to see the hen fluttering in distress in the breeding cage.

My father just stood there looking down at the chicks but there was nothing he could do. As he stooped to pick them up I ran into the house. It wasn't long afterwards I heard the flush of the toilet.

Looking back I suppose that was the turning point. I passed the cages a couple of days later and the seed hoppers and drink fountains were almost empty. I filled them up while my father sat inside reading the football pages.

It was Friday teatime. I was late getting home from a school match and I smelt the cabbage as I opened the door. As soon as I went in I knew there was something wrong. Kenny was sitting at the table eating his dinner, spooning the pieces of cabbage into his mouth. He gagged and swallowed.

"What's wrong, Kenny?" I asked. "What is it?" But he kept on eating.

I went through into the kitchen. My mother was washing the pots, slamming them down on the drainer. She didn't look round.

Then I heard the hammering. I walked past her and opened the back door. My father was down at the far end of the yard. He was kneeling beside a wooden frame about six feet long and two wide and as I watched he removed a nail from between his clenched teeth and hammered it into the frame. There were pieces of timber and tools lying around the yard and a roll of wire mesh leaning against the wall.

He looked up and saw me. He spat out the rest of the nails and with the hand holding the hammer waved at the wooden frame and the roll of wire mesh. He grinned.

"Rabbits," he said.

I turned and looked at my mother. Her lips were pulled so tight they had lost their colour and she slammed a cup down so hard on the draining board the handle came off.

I heard a squeaking sound from beyond her and Kenny came through the doorway into the kitchen. He was pushing the wheels of his chair and as I watched he banged into the doorframe and the chair turned sideways. He pushed again and cleared the opening and then spun round in a complete circle. He managed to straighten up and rolled across the kitchen, bouncing off the cupboard and knocking over a stool. There was panic in his eyes. I tried to stop him as he neared the back door but I wasn't quick enough and he bounced down the step into the yard and almost overturned. As the chair came to a halt he reached down beside him and pulled out his dinner plate and held it out towards my father. "Look, Dada! All finished! Greens all finished!"

And behind him my mother started to sob.

She ran from the kitchen and down the yard to Kenny. She reached over his shoulder and grabbed the plate and flung it at my father. It clipped his ear and shattered against the wall. I stood there, mouth open. I had never seen her this way before.

My father slowly raised his hand to his ear and there was blood on his fingers when he brought it down. He looked at the blood and looked at my mother and then looked at me with a puzzled expression. "What did I do?" he asked.

I went over and stood beside Kenny. He was staring through the shed door at the cage. Big Blue sat on a perch close to the wire, his head bobbing up and down. Kenny lifted his hand towards the bird. "Big Boo," he said.

My mother came over and put her hand on my shoulder and with her other stroked Kenny's cheek and we stood and looked at my father there with the blood running down his neck and I wondered if my mother was thinking the same thing I was thinking for what I was thinking was would I ever be able to trust him again.

THE GRACEFUL WAY OF FLOWERS

Walter was shuffling again. He'd got a lot worse in the past couple of weeks, on occasions almost unable to move forward at all, his feet on the same spot, marking time.

When he'd called for him this morning Emily had been uncomfortable, as though she'd wanted to say something but Walter was with them in the kitchen the whole time. She'd eventually turned back to the sink but not before Norman caught the quiver of her lip, the slow trickle of a tear.

He'd resisted doing it before but today he cupped Walter's elbow in his hand and steered him around the stalls towards the bench seat on the far corner of the square. It was early still, the market not yet in full swing nor would it be for another half-hour or so. Norman liked to get there early to watch the traders setting up but they'd almost missed the bus this morning, what with Walter being so slow and all.

A gentle wind tugged at the flowers in the raised beds around the sides of the square and they swayed slowly, gracefully, holding on to summer's end. Soon they would be gone, replaced by dwarf conifers, heathers, japonica. A green machine chugged and zig-zagged around the cast-iron bollards, picking up the early leaf fall and the debris of last night's takeaways.

A flicker of white caught Norman's attention. A slight figure in a baggy white costume was walking, ballerina-like, across the square towards them. She stopped a little distance away. Her face was alabaster-like, on each cheek a painted tear. Back straight, she hinged down from the waist, laying on the ground a velvet cloth, edges trimmed with beads.

Walter spoke for the first time since they'd got off the bus; "When are we going to see Danny, Norman?... Can we go soon?" He was sitting upright on the seat, face devoid of expression, hands rubbing the tops of his thighs – backwards and forwards, backwards and forwards "...Soon, Norman?"

A balloon-seller, a young man in jeans and body warmer, took up position. Above him helium-filled dolphins and spaceships whipped back and forth beside Teletubbies and Pooh Bears.

Norman answered the way he'd answered last Wednesday and the Wednesday before and the one before that; "I don't know, Walter...It's getting a bit late for this year...It'll be cold out there soon. Maybe next year....In the springtime – the springtime would be best."

Walter nodded. "Can we, Norman? Next year? Can we?...Definitely?" "Yes," said Norman. "Next year.....In the springtime."

"I wonder what he looks like now...I wonder what he looks like now." Walter stared straight ahead, hands rubbing backwards and forwards.

A youth on a skateboard followed the green machine round the bollards. He tilted up the front of the skateboard and tried to spin round but lost control, narrowly missing the ankles of an elderly woman in a woollen winter coat and headscarf and carrying an old-fashioned shopping basket

Norman shot a sideways look at Walter. His hair, white, gossamer-fine, lifted slightly in the breeze. He recalled the black Robert Taylor widow's peak and the girls jostling for position on the dance floor, hoping to catch Walter's eye and Norman, two left feet, trying to remember the sequence, conscious of the look of disdain on his partner's face.....

....."No! No!" The woman clapping her hands, her assistant stopping the record. "Not like that! – Listen to the beat! You have to listen to the beat!...You, there!...Yes, you!...Show him!" And the record starting up again and a grinning Walter gliding past, the girl in his arms eyes closed, hoping the music and the moment would never end.....

A young woman with a child in a pushchair, a toddler by the hand crossed in front of them and stopped at the trinket stall. The sound of an accordion wafted over from somewhere across the square. The girl in the pierrot costume was standing rock still, arms rigid by her side. A passer-by dropped a coin into the cloth by her feet and she suddenly jerked into motion taking three clockwork steps, stopping again with a shudder, feet together, face expressionless, eyes unblinking.

"Left…left…" said Walter.

"What?" said Norman.

The youth on the skateboard hurtled past and Norman pulled his feet in just in time. Walter didn't flinch. "Saskatch … Saskatch…" he said.

"Saskatchewan," said Norman.

"That place," said Walter.

…..Danny. They'd met him at a football game – a Saturday-morning friendly – only it wasn't very. Before the line-up their opponents, a church team, had bowed their heads and said a prayer, then proceeded to kick the daylights out of Walter and Norman's team. There were no linesmen and the referee wore glasses like bottle bottoms and the game was played in a field beside a sheep farm off the Ballygowan Road.

They were a man short, the left-winger down with a bout of gastro-enteritis, the captain scanning the dozen or so spectators asking did anyone fancy a game? And Danny, red hair like a beacon, covering the left field, the winger's kit flapping round him like a shroud.

The ref, who just happened to be the church's senior elder, didn't see the fouls. The church team was clever that way – an elbow here, a set of studs down the shin there and four up by half-time.

Norman, inside-left, got it five minutes into the second half as he went for a loose ball. The church centre-forward shouldered him aside and when the ball bounced out towards the wing followed through with a left jab to Norman's groin.

Norman went down…..

"It's awful far away, Norman. Why did he have to go away there? Why, Norman?"

"For the work, Walter…You ought to know that. We all lost our jobs, you remember…Don't you remember?"

But Walter didn't seem to be listening anymore. He was looking at the pierrot girl but Norman doubted if he could see her from the place where he'd gone.

.....Danny tearing across from the wing, leaping onto the centre-forward's back, wrapping his legs round his waist so he couldn't shake him loose and grabbing him by the hair, sinking his teeth into the centre-forward's left ear.

The blast of the referee's whistle, the chorus of profanities and the church team closing in and Walter and Norman, shoulder to shoulder, ready to slug it out and the church centre-forward twisting and screaming and Danny holding on like a rodeo rider, teeth still locked in his ear.

And afterwards, cold water on swollen eyes, noses plugged with toilet paper and laughing, laughing and slapping shoulders and asking Danny what was he doing tonight and did he fancy going with them to the Oval to see the Glens play Cliftonville that afternoon? And Danny smiling and saying he was going anyway but he'd be at the other goal end.

And a friendship born.

A fanatical Cliftonville supporter, Danny had once played for the reserve team for about twenty minutes until he was sent off for standing on the opposite winger's foot as he was about to jump for a high ball. Saturday night was fight night and although Walter and Norman tried to keep him under control, by the end of that first winter they'd been banned from every dancehall in the city, gradually working their way out towards the towns.....

Norman gazed around the square and tried to recall the first time he'd noticed the change. He supposed, if he really thought about it, there had been signs, gradual things – the forgetfulness which, in truth, he had dismissed at the time, God knows his own memory wasn't great, but there were the other things. Little things – like going missing that time …and the repetition. God, the repetition – especially about Danny when he knew fine well.....

.....Danny walking towards the gangplank, weighed down by the cardboard suitcase and turning to wave and dropping the case and walking quickly back and wrapping his arms round them both and standing there in the March drizzle, holding them and breaking away and grabbing his suitcase and struggling up the gangplank and not looking back.....

The square was busier now, noisier now. A face-painter had set up beside them and several children were forming a queue. The strains of the accordion drifted over the shouts of the traders.

.....Walter urinating against his front gate in full view of a coach load of Japanese tourists and Emily phoning Norman in tears because Mrs Kennedy next door had called round to complain that Walter had told her to piss off when all she'd done was speak to him over the hedge to congratulate him on his display of begonias.....

The pierrot girl jerkily moved again, turning at right angles away from them and stopping with the same shudder, feet apart, head turned to one side as though listening.

"Back...side...together," said Walter, a frown of concentration on his face.

The woman with the two children, the toddler face painted like a kitten, was talking to the balloon seller. He loosened one of the strings and held out Bart Simpson to the toddler and tied a dolphin to the handle of the pushchair.

Walter was hunched forward, deep furrows running across his forehead, hands rubbing backwards, forwards...backwards, forwards...watching the pierrot girl as though anticipating her next clockwork move. She was holding the same position and must have been in some discomfort yet she didn't flinch. She was looking at Norman as if to say; *Please help me*.

Norman rose from his seat. He dug into his trouser pocket and fished out a pound coin and walked over towards the girl. There was very little money in the velvet cloth and he dropped in the coin. Immediately, the girl jerked into motion taking several clockwork steps forward, turned jerkily, walked in the other direction, turned again and came to a halt facing Norman. Her eyes said *thank you* before fading to blank.

Walter's shoelace was undone and Norman bent over and fastened it. He thought of Emily doing this several times a day and of all the other things she would do each day from wiping Walter's mouth to doing up his zip. In spite of it all, Norman knew, she would get up each morning and bath Walter and shave him and dress him and when the time came would toilet him and there would be no complaints.

"He's dead, isn't he?" said Walter. A cluster of leaves, dry, brittle, swirled round their feet.

.....*Par Avion.* Why should it be French and not the universal language of English? Norman thought, slitting open the flimsy blue paper with a finger nail, reading the neat, unfamiliar script...Tripped and fell...gash on side of head...diabetic, maybe you didn't know... septicaemia...He often talked about you...So sorry I never got to meet you.....

He's been dead seven years, for God's sake. Don't you remember, Walter? Can't you remember anything, anymore? I'm tired of hearing the same thing day after day, over and over and over – When are we going to see Danny, Norman? Can we go next year, Norman? Really, Norman? Can we? Can we?

Norman watched as the pierrot girl started walking again, three steps forward, three steps back, stop. "Yes," he said.

The youth on the skateboard was circling a young, plump girl in a hockey outfit, snatching at her games bag. She brushed past him and he called something after her, her face reddening with embarrassment, breaking into a run. The elderly woman dropped a plastic bag of apples into her shopping basket and opened her purse.

"Forward… side…together," said Walter. "Forward…side…together." He pushed himself up, took a couple of steps and stopped. Nodding as if he were counting he crooked his left arm out sideways and raised his right arm in front of him, waist high, bending it at the elbow. Then he began to shuffle and over the shouts of the traders Norman heard the sound of the accordion from the other side of the square… *Somewhere my love…*

Walter moved slowly, awkwardly. Left foot forward a little, right foot coming parallel, left foot closing the space. Right foot forward… left foot… He stopped, lips moving, the pain of concentration.

Norman got up from the seat. People were stopping now, turning, staring. The youth on the skateboard started to point and snigger… and two things happened: the elderly woman's arm came round in a wide arc and the shopping basket caught the youth behind the ear sending him crashing backwards against the vegetable stall and the pierrot girl was walking forward. She seemed to float towards Walter, stopped in front of him. She stood there a brief moment, then fitted her right hand into his left and rested her left hand on his other arm close to his shoulder. Her head came up as far as his chest. Then she leaned backwards slightly and Walter moved with her as she guided him, gently, patiently, and after a while the shuffle disappeared and he was looking down into her eyes, eyes filled with encouragement above the painted tears, and there on the edge of the town square in the mid-morning dying summer air they moved slowly, gracefully in triple time to the sound of the accordion's waltz.

When the music ended there was a loud burst of applause and the girl took Walter by the hand and led him back to his seat. She reached out and touched his cheek and turning away and sweeping up the velvet cloth, walked quickly into the middle of the crowd...and in a moment was gone.

Norman looked at Walter. He was smiling – something Norman hadn't seen in a while. He folded his arms across his chest and sat there with something like triumph on his face. Then he spoke; "Norman, You know what I'd like now, Norman? You know what I'd really like?....."

Walter was shuffling again. Norman ushered him through the doorway of the bus station, thinking; how am I going to explain this to Emily? Two teenage girls were coming towards them and one nudged the other as they passed. The bus was due anytime and over the cries of the children and the singing of the busker and the shuddering revs of the other buses he could hear the tinny background music, the occasional staccato announcement.

Norman guided Walter across to a row of moulded plastic seats and sat him down. He patted his pockets for the tickets.

"Saskatch... Saskatch..." said Walter.

"Saskatchewan," said Norman.

Walter nodded, a puzzled expression on his face as he examined the string wound round his finger. His eyes followed the string up to where Bob the Builder swayed and twisted above his head. He looked down again and began to rub the tops of his thighs. Above him Bob the Builder moved in synchrony.

The bus swept in through the entrance, turned in a wide circle and slowly reversed towards the bay.

Walter raised his hand to the side of his face where the girl had touched him. The string loosened and Bob the Builder rose majestically towards the roof, bumping against the steel purlin, coming to rest with a slight roll in the spiral of heat from the engines. When he lowered his hand the green stripe on his face was smudged across the red into the black.

Emily'll kill me, Norman thought, as he watched the bus come to a halt and the passengers step off. He looked up at Bob the Builder. How long will it stay up there? He imagined in a day or two it would diminish and fall, wizened and limp, to the ground.

He rose and got out the tickets. He reached down for Walter's elbow but Walter took his hand and stood up. Norman, on an impulse, squeezed and felt a slight pressure in return.

They walked towards the bus. The other passengers were rushing to board. Walter spoke; "When can we go over to see Danny, Norman?"

Outside, just beyond the entrance where the crowds scurried about the pedestrian crossing Norman thought he saw a flash of white.

"Next year, Walter...We'll go next year...In the springtime... Definitely."

SOUP OF THE DAY: PART DEUX

Belfast, 5 years later

Mrs Johnston turned sideways and cast an admiring glance at her reflection in Ann Summers's window.

She was well pleased with her implants. Almost as pleased as she was with her remodelled *derriere*. In that respect she was glad she had gone for the Jennifer Lopez and now, what with the neck lift, the liposuction, the waxing (tucked, sucked and plucked, you might say), she was completely unrecognisable from the rather dowdy Mrs Johnston of five years ago.

Mr Johnston, too, was completely unrecognisable. Since that awful night he had undergone a total physical and spiritual transformation. Having spent the years since his divorce at a Benedictine retreat, he had now joined the Hare Krishna movement. Resplendent now in a bright orange robe, head shaven, he shook his tambourine and watched the others dance in a circle on the pavement outside Tesco, his ex-wife, unknown to him, a mere thirty yards away on the other side of the street. *Quelle coincidence.*

Mandy Murphy, on the other hand, was completely recognizable. Since the events of five years ago she hadn't changed a bit if you didn't count the tattoo on the side of her neck and the ring through her left nostril. Accompanied by her two sisters, Mandy Murphy was in town buying a new pair of combat boots, having tried unsuccessfully to remove the bloodstains from her old ones. Mandy Murphy was a big strapping girl and her two sisters were big strapping girls. *Tres formidable*, you might say. Mandy Murphy and her sisters could have held the pass at Thermopylae.

Mrs Johnston browsed over the items in Ann Summer's window. She rather fancied the red basque with the black lace. She wondered if Ahmed would like it, not for himself of course, but she thought if she bought it, it might cheer him up a bit – he'd seemed somewhat listless of late but she'd put it down to too many figs in his diet. Across the road, outside Tesco, a group of men dressed in orange were dancing in a circle. Another was standing watching. He glanced over at her and she patted her hair demurely. She looked again at the basque. Go for it, Yolande, she thought and pushed open the door.

Mr Johnston banged rhythmically on his tambourine. Across the road a woman was looking at him. She turned and went into a shop. Suddenly, he had a compulsion to join in with his companions and when a gap appeared he merged in with the others and began to dance. It was not a pretty sight. As he hopped and skipped he had a tendency to throw out his left leg (a legacy of that night), forcing him to apologize to the man in front every time he kicked him up the backside. The more Mr Johnston danced, the more enthusiastic he got. He whirled and chanted and rattled his tambourine like a man possessed.

Britney McGimpsey didn't want a strawberry lolly. Britney McGimpsey, seven years old, wanted a chocolate lolly and she was making sure everyone within a hundred yards in any direction knew about it.

Britney McGimpsey's mother didn't give a rat's ass what Britney wanted. She'd just bought her a strawberry lolly and a strawberry lolly was all she was getting.

Britney promptly flung the lolly away, whereupon her mother, just as promptly, whacked her round the back of the head. But no one saw this as all attention was diverted to what happened next.

It was quite spectacular, really. The lolly landed on the ground just as Mr Johnston's size twelve Roman sandal came down. Already at full throttle, Mr Johnston hurtled forward. Dropping his tambourine, he thrust out both hands, fingers splayed, seeking something, anything at all, to stop his forward momentum.

His luck was in – or just about to run out, depending on how you look at it, *mes amis.*

Mandy Murphy's powers had not diminished over the intervening years. She saw beyond the shaven head, the orange robe, the sunken eyes now taking on a haunted look.

"You!" she hissed.

Mr Johnston, loins girded up, sprinted along Royal Avenue, three big women in hot pursuit. As he passed Castle Court a little man in a flat cap held out a leaflet. "The end is coming!" he shouted.

"So's bloody Mandy Murphy!" Mr Johnston shouted back as he dodged through the traffic and legged it away in the direction of York Street.

Britney McGimpsey, in a demonstration of the breadth of her knowledge of children's rights, told her mother she was going to report her to Social Services. Britney's mother, in a demonstration of the depth of her maternal instincts, gave Britney another whack round the back of the head.

Mrs Johnston came out of Ann Summers's carrying a shopping bag. A young woman trailed a little girl past, shouting something about ice lollies. Across the road there seemed to be some sort of commotion, but she was already thinking about the evening ahead. Ahmed would be pleased. Ah, she thought, isn't life wonderful? She still had a little money left from the divorce settlement – enough for a further little indulgence or two. A session of colonic irrigation, perhaps? She sighed contentedly as she walked jauntily towards the taxi stand, thinking; I wonder what it would be like to bathe in goat's milk……

Mandy Murphy took her new boots back to the shop as they were too tight across the toes. The man in the shop suggested to her that she stuff some wet newspaper in them. She told him that she had a better idea and suggested to him that he stuff his boots where the sun didn't shine.

Britney McGimpsey now has a little baby brother, just three weeks old. His name is Wayne. Britney's father, who, some time ago, in a demonstration of the height of his ineptitude, fell fifteen feet while nicking the lead off a church roof, is currently serving out the last couple of weeks of a twelve-month sentence at Meghaberry.

Boy is he in for a surprise when he gets out!

Mr Johnston is no longer a member of the Hare Krishna movement. He is now a Seventh Day Adventist and has left a note for the milkman telling him not to make any more deliveries after Thursday of next week.

Mrs Johnston has spent all her divorce settlement. She is not, however, overly concerned as Ahmed seems to always have a ready supply of cash these days. This all coincided with him fitting a lock to the spare bedroom door and keeping the key. There has also been a corresponding and dramatic rise in the electricity bill. Ahmed says he has delicate computer equipment in the room but there is a funny smell coming from somewhere and she has never heard of computer equipment that needs watering every day.

It's all really rather odd.

IN BOTANIC AVENUE

Belfast, 2012

When I first saw him he was lying in a shop doorway, the water siphoning up the hem of his overcoat. The thing is, all he had to do was move to the next doorway and he would have been on a four-inch step and clear of the floodwater which had spread into a lake in the dip in the road above the station entrance.

It had just stopped raining for the first time in over thirty-six hours and the late February wind was whipping up miniature waves across the surface of the road. It would be a couple more hours at least before the flooding subsided and ahead of me, just this side of the traffic lights, three men in yellow jackets were working to unblock the ducting at the kerb edge.

As I drew level with the sleeping man I hesitated. He lay on his side, curled like a foetus, back to the world, head resting against the doorframe. All I could see was a shock of copper-coloured hair, matted, spiky with dirt and damp. He gave a jerk, snorted and settled down again like a dog settles down, oblivious to the morning bite and the water soaking into his clothes. I stood there a moment trying to decide if I should wake him but I was already running late and I turned and continued on my way, trying to walk on my heels, heading for higher ground.

When I saw him again he was working the other side of the street. It was a day or so later and I was just leaving the station. The roads had dried out by then and so had he. He was bigger than he had looked in the shop doorway and his hair glinted in the weak sun, the way it had all those years ago. I stopped short and a student, it looked like, bumped into me, brushing past in exasperation.

I stared across the road, through the gaps in the stream of traffic. He was standing in the middle of the pavement, holding out a plastic cup and I watched the passers-by give him a wide berth, looking elsewhere but into his face.

From where I stood Eberhart hadn't changed that much. A little thinner, maybe, but that was all. His black topcoat was ripped at the pockets and what appeared to be a scorch mark ran diagonally from shoulder to waist. He was unshaven and unkempt, but he still had that bull-like stance, head thrust forward, big rounded shoulders.....

....."The Jameson Raid, Scott – When was it?"

No hesitation: "Eighteen ninety-five, Sir."

He would nod. Slowly. Reluctantly. He didn't like it. He didn't like it one bit.

Dates came easily to me. Wars especially. I suppose I was blessed with a good memory – a gift, someone said. Pity it didn't extend to languages or mathematics or chemistry. Dates, however…

But Eberhart persisted. In the middle of a lesson he would suddenly swing round, hunch those big shoulders, focus his baleful eyes on me; "Dates of the Indian Mutiny, Scott – start and finish?"

"Eighteen fifty-seven, Sir – May – until eighteen fifty-eight." Pause. Then… "July."

And he would glare at me, turn away. Some day…some day…

It went on for the whole of that, my final, year: "The storming of the Bastille, Scott?"…An easy one. "The Battle of Stamford Bridge?...The revolt of Perkin Warbeck? …When was the Second Boer War, Scott?"

On and on it went. I couldn't understand why – why he singled me out. When I was leaving, my last day, 1987 it was, I sought him out. He was alone in the room, hunched over his desk. He looked up. "What do you want, Scott?"

"I want to ask you something." No *Sir.* My last day and it didn't matter anymore. "What did I ever do to you? Why did you pick on me all the time?"

He pushed back his chair, clasped his big hands across his stomach, laughed – a humourless laugh, contemptuous. "It's like this, Scott, I just don't like you – it's that simple. I don't like you and I never have. Don't ask me to explain because there is no explanation – it's an instinctive thing." And he turned his back on me and resumed whatever it was he had been doing.

Eighteen… I was eighteen. I held back the tears until I was alone…..

I could have crossed the road, walked up to him, standing there on the pavement, hair like a wild man, clothes stained, torn, begging for loose change, said; "Remember me, Mr Eberhart…*Sir?*"

I walked away.

I was late leaving the office that night and missed the five-thirty. Almost half an hour to kill until the next train, I went for a cup of coffee.

The restaurant was almost opposite the station entrance and through the window I saw them coming down the street. It was nearly dark but the bull-like shape was unmistakable, walking down towards the square, clutching the paper parcel, bottle neck protruding. He was on the outside, the woman, in a shapeless track suit, in the middle, on the inside a tall thin man in a donkey jacket and watch cap. The thin man had a slight sideways walk, exaggerated by the swing of arms that extended well beyond the limits of his sleeves. He spoke across to Eberhart and Eberhart passed the bottle over. The thin man tilted it to his mouth and then held it out Eberhart but the woman intercepted it and took a long drink before Eberhart snatched it away, holding it tight to his chest as they continued down the street.

I didn't see him the next morning or the one after. On the following Monday I turned out of the station and walked straight into him.

He was standing in the middle of the pavement, holding out the plastic cup. He looked right into my face. He spoke; "Could you spare a few pence for a cup of tea, Sir?" *Sir.* His eyes, watery from the cold wind, still held that baleful look of old.

People change. I could see, close up, that he'd aged. He would be over sixty now, I reckoned.

I, too, had changed, my hair greying now, a little sparser, a mustache. I'd filled out a bit, glasses. I lowered my head anyway, dug into my pocket, dropped a pound coin into the cup.

"Thank you, Sir – God bless you, Sir." But even in those words the touch of arrogance.

I took a chance, looked straight into his eyes, held the look. But there was nothing. I nodded, stepped round him. A few paces on I glanced back. He was still standing there, facing the other way, head thrust forward, coat flapping in the wind.

"Jeremy's getting married next week, Mr Scott. We're having a whip round for a present." Hanna laid the envelope on my desk. "Would you like to contribute?"

Hanna worked upstairs. She and Jeremy had started around the same time. I liked Hanna. Jeremy, too – a good worker, a pleasant way with him.

"Of course." I fished out a fiver and slid it into the envelope.

"Thanks very much. I've caught everybody now except Mr McEvoy. Is he in?"

"He's at a seminar – back tomorrow."

"Would you mention it to him?"

I nodded. "I'll see him first thing."

He was there again that evening. He was sitting on a rock at the corner of the waste ground, slumped forward, bottle in his lap, muttering to himself. I walked past, stopped, turned back, went over. I reached for my wallet, took out a fiver for the second time that day and tucked it into the pocket of his coat. He lifted his head and our eyes met again. But again there was nothing. I tried to think of something to say but couldn't. His head drooped forward again to his chest.

"Goodnight," I said and walked on.

"I'd rather not," said Jack McEvoy.

"Huh?" I looked at him in surprise.

"I'd rather not contribute."

"Why? Has Jeremy done something to you?"

"No."

"But why, then, Jack?...You must have some reason."

"No – I don't have a reason. I just don't like him, that's all...It's an instinctive thing."

I sat back in my chair. A couple of the others, sensing something, glanced across.

I stared at Jack McEvoy. We'd worked together for nearly twelve years. We played golf every Saturday. I was godfather to his eldest boy. When I'd turned the car over three years ago and ended up in hospital with my leg on a pulley, he'd driven my wife over every night and twice on Sunday for three weeks. We confided in each other, Jack and I. We sensed one another's moods, talked each other out of them. So, I could have taken it further, tried to discuss it, told him I thought he was being a little unreasonable, said; Hey, Jack, don't you think you're being a bit unfair, here?

But only two words came to mind.

So I said them.

I heard the commotion when I was in the newsagents. I paid the girl and walked to the door.

The man with the long arms passed me at a clumsy trot, heading up the hill, eyes filled with alarm. I looked down in the direction he had come and saw the flashing blue light and the people starting to gather.

By the time I reached the fringe of the crowd they were bringing him out. It took three of them. I looked beyond him into the off-licence at the broken bottles, several of them, the wet, slippery floor. A shop assistant was trundling in a wheelie bin, a mop protruding.

Eberhart struggled, swore, trying to pull free and for a brief moment his eyes found mine before they frogmarched him across the pavement and bundled him into the back of the landrover. I watched them manhandle him onto the seat. A policeman got in either side and the third reached for the door handle.

Then I heard it – coming from the back of the landrover, over the noise of the traffic; "When was the War of Jenkin's Ear?"

...The years rolling back like film credits......Seventeen...Seventeen...

Seventeen-thirty-nine.

The policeman was closing the door.

"Seventeen-thirty…seven!" I shouted.

I heard the roar…triumphant; "Hah!...Got you, Scott!... Got you!...*Got you!*"

And the door slammed shut and the policeman climbed into the front, the landrover growled away from the kerb, edged into the mainstream traffic and rumbled slowly up the road.

When I arrived home I got on the phone, called in a couple of favours, found out where they were holding him. He was to be charged in the morning. But it was well into the next day by the time I got the chance to phone again.

"Eberhart?...Oh, yes…The off-licence… He's gone. He was released… They made full restitution for the damage…All his drinking buddies. God knows how they managed to do it. One guy, arms down near his knees, you shoulda seen him, came in with a plastic bag full of coins. They must have been out there on the streets all night. I'm surprised they didn't blow the lot on drink. The guy brought it in was stone-cold sober, though, but he was shaking. God, was he shaking. Paid the owner every penny and the charge was dropped on the condition Eberhart stayed away from the area… Where is he now? I've really no idea…No idea at all…"

It was blowing cold again with more rain on the way as I walked up the street towards the patch of waste ground beyond the traffic lights. There were few people about. It was too late to be going anywhere, too soon to be coming back.

I sat the long package upright on top of one of the rocks and in the corner of my eye saw a slight movement in the shadows of the entry at the far corner of the waste ground. I crossed the street to the university side and waited.

There were five of them – three men, two women. They emerged slowly, one after the other, and shuffled towards the rock, the man with the long arms in the lead. He reached out, touched the package, picked it up. He pulled out the bottle and turned the label towards the glow of the street lamp. The others clustered round. He turned and looked across the road at me and I thought I saw him nod. Then he slipped the bottle under his coat and one by one they melted back into the shadows.

I stood on until the rain came, until the first heavy drop hit me on the cheek, then I tugged up my collar and turning my back to the wind, walked quickly up the street towards the bright lights of the station.

OCTOBER DAWN

Belfast, 1966

He woke to the feel of the hand on his shoulder. He shrugged it off, mumbled something incoherent.

"Time to get up," his father said.

"What?…What for?…Sure it's Sunday." His voice sullen through the half-sleep.

"You said you'd take me down."

"Take you…" The half-remembered promise in a moment of recklessness, no thought given to the earliness of the hour, the forfeiture of a long lie-in. Now the cold realisation of what he had said the day before.

"Well, you still don't have to, you know…Not if you don't want to." The older man turned towards the door.

"No…No…It's all right…I'll be down in a minute." He pushed himself up, reluctant to leave the warmth of the bed, and sat on the edge, wrapping his arms round himself, shivering, the October dawn just starting to filter through the gap in the curtains.

The little Austin was twelve years old and had seen better times but it was the best he could afford and he had only had it since the beginning of the week. In spite of its age the engine responded right away to the pull of the starter and he moved off from the kerb, the windscreen misting over almost immediately. He tugged down his cuff and wiped the glass clear with his forearm.

"You were brave and late last night," said his father.

Aw, hear we go, he thought. *What took him so long? Nineteen and he still talks to me like I'm a child.*

They left the maze of side streets, encountering more traffic now although it was still too early for the bus service. Most of the other cars were heading the same way as them and, only a matter of weeks since his test, he drove cautiously.

"She runs all right," said the older man.

"She's not too bad," he replied. The lights at the junction changed to amber and he slowed down, stopped. There was a silence in the car and he was starting to feel the tension already. *It's got to be we've nothing to say to each other. You'd think now there's only the two of us he'd try at least to have some sort of conversation with me. I can't be bothered, anymore – I'm going to look for a place of my own. Maybe by the summer...as soon as I get a bit more money gathered up.*

His father started to cough, that old hard, wracking sound. *Oh, God, not again*, thought the young man – *that's another thing I wouldn't miss.* The older man hunched forward, shoulders heaving with the effort, then the coughing eased, stopping as suddenly as it had begun, leaving him breathing heavily, arms stiff, hands braced on his knees.

Should I? Should I ask? Then; "Are you all right?"

His father cleared his throat once more and nodded. "I'm okay...Turn in next on the right and go down to the end and over the bridge."

There were a lot of men now, walking briskly most of them, heads down, lunch boxes under their arms. *They all look the same – just like him.*

He needed to slow down there were so many people about. A cyclist wobbled in front of him forcing him to brake sharply. They were inside the harbour estate now, huts and long workshops either side, cranes and gantries projecting high above the rooftops. A lone seagull hovered in the distance, swooping, dropping out of view.

"Go right down to the end and round to your left," said his father.

He drove slowly, eyes darting side to side, mindful of the throng of men all about him. *What a depressing place. How could anyone want to work here?* It was starting to drizzle and everywhere was cold-cement

140

grey.

"Just round the far end there and find a place to stop," said the older man.

He did as he was instructed, turned the corner and saw the rig.

He had known about it, of course, had seen the beginnings on television, but he was still unprepared for the sheer magnitude of the structure. Like some awesome Wellsian creation it loomed there, three hundred feet high, its great seamed and studded tubular legs straddling the dockside.

His father opened the door. "Righto, then…I suppose I'll hardly see you tonight?"

The young man was still staring up at the rig. "What? …Oh…Maybe…" He looked out at his father standing at the side of the car. "Where do you work?"

"Me?…Up there." The older man pointed towards the top of the rig, barely visible through the morning mist.

"Up there?" He looked at his father in disbelief. "How do you get up?"

"Oh, a winch sometimes. Sometimes I have to climb the ladder. It can take a while…I stop now and then for a rest."

"I never realised…Do you really have to? …Go up there?"

"I've no choice…That's where the job is…What else can I do?" All of a sudden he seemed awkward, searching for something else to say. Finally; "Maybe I will see you later then, okay?" He turned and walked away.

The young man sat on for a moment then looked over his shoulder to check it was safe to reverse. He saw the flask on the back seat. He grabbed it, jumped out. "Hey! Wait! Wait a minute, Dad!"

His father stopped, looked back.

"You forgot this." He ran over and handed the flask to him.

"Good job you noticed," said his father. There was a pause; "Thanks."

"What time do you stop?"

"Five…Why?"

"It's just…I'll pick you up."

"You don't need…" The older man stopped … "All right," he said.

"Ok, then…five o'clock?"

"Five o'clock it is," said his father.

They stood looking at each other for a moment then a horn started to blare. His father walked away, lunch box and flask tucked under one arm.

When he had gone a few steps he turned and said something but the young man couldn't make it out. He watched him move off again, a little stiffly at first, but then his step lightened a little. The young man gazed up again towards the top of the rig, glinting dully through the mist, and when he looked down again his father was nowhere to be seen, lost in the crowd.

LAST SUMMER

Cotswolds, 1999

Afterwards, looking back, thinking it through, he knew he should have accepted it long before the Chipping Norton thing.

She had taken to long bouts of silence, to spending a lot of time in her room, to wandering off on her own. The enthusiasm of youth consigned to the past, it seemed like she was floating away from him, borne on a breeze of indifference, and although he realised now that he should have let go he had chosen to ignore the signs, to evict the thought from his mind; *She's not much more than a child, she still needs to be with us. She still needs me...doesn't she?*

The cottage was tucked in behind a row of elders some half a mile from the main road and all the brochure had promised. It had been Judy's choice this year; "Let's go to the Wye Valley – we've never gone that far south."

For the past five or so years they'd taken turns to pick the destination. Now that Karen was old enough they had to be careful to sew the seeds, make her think it was her idea – ever since the year she'd suggested Grangemouth. "But it's such a nice name," she'd said.

He emerged from the bedroom and did a half-turn, arms outstretched. "What do you think?"

"Where on earth did you get those?"

"Bought them last week – Do you like them?"

"They're kind of…kind of…" her voice trailed away.

"You don't like them?"

"Aren't they a bit over the top for somebody your…?"

"Go on … say it…somebody my age. I don't care – anyway, nobody knows me here."

"Thank God," she muttered.

He made a pretence of being offended, then; "Where'd Karen go?"

"Out to check the tennis court…Michael, have you noticed anything about her lately?"

He feigned ignorance. "Like what?"

"She's got very withdrawn …It's not like her at all."

"I wouldn't worry about her – You know what kids can be like."

"She's almost sixteen, Michael – hardly a kid anymore."

His daughter passed the window. As she came through the doorway he adopted the same pose as before. She stood there looking at his trousers then she looked at her mother. Her face said it all.

"Well…Okay, then…These cost me nearly seventeen quid, you know."

"No kidding," said Judy.

"You'd better get used to them – I've only these and my grey cords with me and it's too hot for them."

It was hot. Even now, well into the evening, there was no sign of a drop in temperature. The sun had beaten down on them throughout the journey, the tarmac melting on the roads, sticking to the wheel arches of the car. "Keep on collecting it at this rate and we'll have enough to do the driveway when we get home," Michael had said.

"What's the tennis court like?" asked Judy. Use of it was part of the package.

"Not bad," replied Karen. She went over to the television, examined the controls, switched it on.

"Maybe we'll get a game tomorrow – when we've had a night's rest." Judy looked at Michael, rolled her eyes and went into the bedroom to finish unpacking.

Michael slapped at the fold lines in his trousers.

Gloucester and Beatrix Potter. Stroud and Laurie Lee. Bath. The Forest of Dean – the first week went by.

Karen remained withdrawn, introspective. Michael watched her from the corners of his eyes. The only thing that seemed to raise any enthusiasm was the daily game of tennis with Judy.

And all the time the heat was intense – open windows, cool air fan on maximum, steering wheel burning the palms of the hands.

"Hey, listen to this," he said. "According to the paper this was the hottest place yesterday in the whole of the British Isles." He sat on the river bank, trousers rolled up, feet in the water, newspaper on his knee. Something blotted out the sun and he glanced up. A blue and yellow hot-air balloon swept high overhead, the burner hissing and plopping, coloured streamers trailing from the basket. Over towards the town a group of men was unfolding the silk of another. He set the newspaper aside. "Fancy a game of tennis?"

Judy, beside him, pushed up her sunglasses. "You haven't played tennis in fifteen years."

"So? I've decided to get fit again – really fit, I mean. I've been thinking about a lot of things lately. Things like I sit around too much. Got to keep middle age at bay, right? – Bit of squash…Bit of jogging…"

"Do you want to give yourself a heart attack?"

He was slow to reply. When he did his voice was different; "I thought if I did all these things I could maybe spend a little more time with her…with Karen. She's growing too quickly for me…I…" His voice trailed away.

Judy reached out, touched his hand. "Michael, you can't change these things…You can't stop her growing up…Just the same as you can't start growing young again."

He nodded, turned his head away so she wouldn't see his face and gazed upriver.

Stratford-Upon-Avon and Shakespeare. The Malvern Hills and Elgar. Worcester. Well into the second week now and always, always, the hot, merciless sun.

"Look! There's another one!" The rabbit lay on the verge. "That must be the fifth since we came onto this road – you'd think people were trying to hit them!" Karen was clearly upset.

"They get hypnotised by the car headlamps and freeze, I've heard." Michael concentrated on the bends in the road.

"There's the tennis ball." Judy pointed. They'd lost it the previous day.

Michael looked across into the neighbouring field and saw it half-hidden by a fallen branch.

"I'll get it." He trotted back to a gap in the fence where the middle strand was missing and ducked through. Judy pointed again and he found the ball and stuffed it into his trouser pocket.

He hesitated, looked back at the gap and made instead for the nearest support post. The wire had been renewed here and the barbs of the top strand, chest high, glinted in the early-evening sun. He pulled himself up shakily, holding the post with both hands.

"Mind your trousers," Judy warned as he threw one leg over, placing his foot between the barbs.

The wire wobbled and he gripped the top of the post. "At this precise moment it's not my trousers I'm worried about." He carefully brought his other leg over and lowered himself to the grass, more than a little relieved.

He took Judy's hand and they sidestepped down the slope to the river bank. A solitary fisherman sat, hunched over, watching the river bed for movement. A magpie fluttered out of a tree. Beyond the far meadow a balloon, red and white stripes, began its ascent, slowly, majestically. Even at that distance they could see the flame, hear the hiss of the burner as it swept away over the town.

"It's so peaceful here," said Judy.

"It was a good choice this year." He reached out, drew her close and the tennis ball dropped from his pocket, bounced and splashed into the water. It bobbed up immediately and they watched the current carry it downstream.

Chipping Norton was a mistake… But how was I to know?

They had spent most of the afternoon in Stow-In-The-Wold and it was early yet – too early to return to the cottage.

"Let's go to Chipping Norton. Whatisname – used to be on television – is supposed to have a shop there. It's not far." Judy had the map on her knees. "It's our last day. It would be a shame to come all this way and not visit it. These places have such lovely names…"

It was a half hour or so before closing time when they got there. They turned left into the wide main street, drove past the shops and almost immediately found themselves approaching the outskirts. The only people they could see were a man and a woman standing in a doorway, the woman's arm linked through that of the man.

"Looks like the town centre's the other way." Judy looked behind her.

Michael drove on to a mini-roundabout and circled back the way they had come. "Not many parking spaces," he said. Both sides of the street were lined with cars yet there were hardly any people.

The street divided ahead of him, the left fork branching off on a slope. Michael slowed, undecided which way to go and the couple from a moment ago suddenly appeared at his offside wing. He braked sharply and skirted round them, taking the left fork. The man glared at him.

He drove a little way up the incline, saw a space behind a Volkswagen and it took a minute to manoeuvre in. He stretched his arms and peered out past Karen. They were opposite an antique shop. He opened the door, eased himself stiffly out of his seat and stood there, arching his back.

"Hey!" he heard.

He turned.

The man and woman were standing there, the woman tugging at the man's arm. He brushed her roughly aside. He was a little over medium height, broad. He wore a tee shirt, stained, stretched over a beer belly. His hair was cropped close and he had an earring in his left ear. There was a tattoo of some kind on his neck below the earring and more on his forearms. His face gleamed with sweat.

He leaned towards Michael. "If you try to run me down again I'll break your bloody neck."

In spite of the heat of the sun Michael felt a chill. The man swayed slightly. Michael threw a glance up the street. The nearest person was a good fifty yards away, walking in the opposite direction. Karen was just getting out of the front seat and tipping it forward for Judy. She turned, sensing something.

The woman pulled at the man's arm again. Again he shook her off. He stepped forward, raised his finger until it was a couple of inches from Michael's eyes. "Hear me? Do that again and I'll smash your head in!"

*Do what? You've got this all wrong! I didn't…*The words were in his head and he was about to say them when he saw the look in the man's eyes. The look said; *Go on…go ahead…* and Michael knew. *He wants me to respond…he wants me to… so… that…*

147

The man was still staring at him, pale washed-out eyes. He ran his tongue across his lips, waiting. Hoping. Michael risked another glance up the street but there was no-one at all about now. He looked back into the man's face and away and sideways and down and down until his eyes focussed on the ground somewhere near the man's feet. He swallowed. "I'm sorry," he mumbled.

The woman said something to the man and pulled at him again. He stood there a moment, still swaying, then backed away, disappointed. "Smash his bloody head in." He stumbled off, the woman gripping his arm.

Michael began to breath in short, sharp gulps. He was having trouble getting air in. He looked across the car roof at Karen. Their eyes met and they stood like that for a moment, facing one another. Then he turned away.

"What was that all about?" Judy was out of the car now, looking after the man and woman, puzzled.

"Nothing…a drunk… that's all… Just a drunk." Michael crossed over to the antique shop. A pine apothecary cabinet filled most of the back of the window display. In front of it stood a rack of willow-pattern plates and a pair of silver candlesticks. There was an oil lamp and a selection of snuff boxes. There were two bronze statuettes and a trinket box and a flat iron on a stand. There was a boot scraper and an abacus with faded beads. There were dolls and clocks, a white five-pound note in a frame, a moustache cup, a flintlock pistol, a copper hearth rail, a candle snuffer, a long-handled bed warmer, two china dogs… postcards…

He didn't see any of them.

What he saw was the look on his daughter's face.

He drove at a steady fifty miles an hour. He always drove at fifty when something was bothering him. Judy, twenty years of marriage, recognised the signs and sat quietly in the back seat. Karen, too, was silent.

At one point he reached across and switched on the radio. Bette Midler – *The Wind Beneath My Wings*. The sun dipped into the tree line and he flicked on the headlights, put them on dip. He leaned forward, switched off the radio. The needle hovered around fifty, cool-air fan on high, the steady hum of wheels.

It gave him no chance.

It appeared from his offside, trying to make the verge by the light of the headlamps. Beside him, Karen screamed but there wasn't a thing he could do. The front grill caught it fair and square, a sickening thud.

Judy yelled, "What is it?... What's happened?"

"A rabbit! I've hit a rabbit!" *I've never hit anything before.* He was braking now and in his mirror, in the half-light, he could see the rabbit jerking, twisting in the middle of the road.

He pulled the car part-way onto the verge and switched off the engine. He fumbled for the seat-belt buckle, released it, threw open the door, slammed it shut. He looked back along the road at the writhing shape.

He broke into a run. The rabbit was trying to drag itself towards the sanctuary of the verge.

Do something, for God's sake! Do something! He looked round. He recalled passing a laneway twenty or thirty yards back and a dry stone wall.

He started to run again. *I've never hit anything before.* One of his ankles gave under him on the uneven surface of the laneway. He tugged at the top row of stones until he found a loose one and it came away in a shower of dust. He hobbled back, out of breath, holding the stone in both hands. He could see Judy and beyond her, Karen, watching him through the back window.

He reached where the rabbit had been. A thick smear of something led to the road edge. A rustling noise came from the undergrowth where the bank dipped away and he scrambled down towards it, hunched forward, peering side to side, the stone cradled in his arms.

The rabbit lay on its side. It squirmed, tried to get away. He knelt beside it, raised the stone. The rabbit turned its eyes up to him. Bette Midler sang in his head, something about heroes. He closed his eyes and swung the stone down hard.

He levered himself up, wincing from the pain in his ankle, turned, a wave of dizziness. He wiped his hands on his trousers and they came away sticky. He looked down at the dark patch over one knee and felt the wetness through the light material.

He pulled himself back up towards the road. A bus was approaching. The driver slowed on seeing the car and a row of curious faces peered out at him. The bus pulled out past and continued on its way, gathering speed.

He eased himself into the car, sat for a moment staring out of the windscreen and started the engine, glancing in the mirror. Karen's hands were clenched tightly in her lap. He fastened his belt, pulled slowly away, keeping the speed just under thirty. No one spoke.

It was dark all of a sudden and he put the lights on full beam, leaning forward, eyes darting side to side, scanning the verges, searching for movement, leg muscles tense in readiness. "I've never killed anything before," he said and in the back Judy began to sob.

He sat on the river bank and watched a family of ducks weaving through the reeds close to the far side – one adult and five little ones. It was quiet except for the occasional plop as a fish rose to snatch an insect from the surface, the intermittent hiss of the burner of an early-morning balloon high overhead and reflected in the water below.

So peaceful, he thought.

"Dad?"

He turned. He hadn't heard her approach.

"Mum says everything's packed and breakfast will be ready in a few minutes."

"Ok – I'll be up in a minute." He looked across the river. The ducks were approaching an outcrop on the far bank.

"Dad?"

"Yes?"

There was a silence. He turned to her. *God, but she's getting tall.*

"I thought…" Hesitation… then; "I want you to know I won't be coming with you next year."

He looked away. "I know," he said. *Why do ducks always swim in a line?*

"It's just…I'll soon be sixteen, Dad…I want to be with my friends… people my own age…Do other things…See other places…"

"It's okay," he said…. "It's okay." He tried to smile.

She touched his shoulder, her hand warm through his shirt. Her voice, when she spoke again, shook a little; "Come up soon…I'd like you to come up soon."

He nodded, turned back to the river. The ducks had gone and the balloon was high and away over the town. The river surface rippled, a series of rings spreading out below him. He stared into the water.

In a while he stood and slapped at the seat of his cords and slowly began to climb the hill.

DEEP AND CRISP AND EVEN

Belfast, sometime in the early 1960s

The bookies were laying ten to one against snow that year.

I can't remember whose idea it was but it was getting close to midnight, the bar long since closed, the waiters looking at their watches. We had gone through all the songs and things were starting to fall a little flat when somebody said; "Why don't we go and see Harry?"

So we spilt outside and piled into the cars. I was a nominated driver – me and Greg and Victor. But for someone who wasn't supposed to be drinking, Greg was the noisiest and clumsiest of the lot of us.

Victor was driving a Vauxhall and Greg had his father's Rover and I brought up the rear in a seven-year-old Ford Prefect with a dickey starter and nine payments to go.

I had Norman and Julie in the back, Amy beside me. Amy was blonde, not long started in the typing pool and had been sending me signals all evening. For obvious reasons, therefore, I wasn't in favour of prolonging the festivities any longer than necessary. Anyway I couldn't see the point in driving nearly eight miles to call on somebody I didn't particularly like and who was probably by that time tucked up in bed.

Harry? Harry worked in a little box of an office in the corner of the accounts department behind a pile of ledgers, calculator rolls and balance sheets covered in his neat little figures. He was older than the rest of us by quite a bit and whereas we spent our lunch breaks in the cloakroom playing poker, Harry would hide himself away in his office studying the financial markets. He wasn't married, that much we knew, but any attempt to quiz him about his private life came to nothing.

My heater fan was high in noise level and low in efficacy and every now and then I had to wipe the mist off the windscreen. The others started singing Christmas songs. Me? – I get melancholy at Christmas. Sometimes I wish I could fall asleep on Christmas Eve and stay that way until the day after Boxing Day. But I joined in anyway rather than spoil my chances with Amy who nudged against me more than necessary, I thought, each time we made a left turn.

Before we had gone three miles we'd been left behind. I tried pushing up the speed but the car wasn't having any of it, the engine misfiring, the steering wheel vibrating forcing me to slow down. When we came off the dual carriageway the others were waiting and we set off again, Greg in the lead, insisting he knew the way.

Fifteen minutes later and I was fed up. I was on the point of suggesting we call the whole thing off and leave the others to it, when, ahead of me, Victor slowed down and beyond him Greg's car turned into a high-hedged avenue. I found myself climbing a hill flanked by old three-story terrace houses.

Greg pulled over and stopped and we drew in behind in convoy. Greg got out and, a little unsteadily it seemed to me, went over to a gate, opened it and went along a narrow path to a door. We all followed and he motioned to us to gather round, murmuring instructions. Then he pressed the bell.

I looked around. The curtains were drawn but there was a lamp above the door, the paintwork blistered, mortar crumbling between the bricks.

As Greg reached again for the bell a light shot out from the transom. We shuffled into position, Amy giggling.

The door opened a fraction and Harry's head poked out.

"Merry Christmas, Harry!" we yelled and burst into Good King Wenceslas. Greg gave the door a shove and, still singing, we bundled past a bewildered Harry into the long hall, a doorway at the far end and what looked like a kitchen beyond. He shouted a protest but by that time we were all milling around the foot of the narrow staircase.

The hall was dimly lit, large-patterned faded paper covering the walls.

Where these met the ceiling there was an old ornate cornice, pieces broken off here and there. The carpet was frayed, curling along the edge. The whole place exuded gloom.

Harry reached over and closed a partly-open door. He was clearly nervous.

"Well, Harry – Glad to see us?" shouted Greg. "Thought we'd drop in! – Bring you a spot of Christmas spirit!" He produced a half-full bottle from under his coat. "Get the glasses out and we'll get a few songs going!" He looked round. "Try and liven this place up a bit... looks like it could do with it."

"I don't drink, Greg – you know that." Harry replied. "Anyway, this isn't convenient... I'm...I'm a bit busy right now..."

"Come on, Harry! – Let your hair down. Everybody has a drink at Christmas. Go and find some glasses, somebody."

Norman pushed through into the kitchen and I heard the sound of cupboard doors opening, then a crash. "Oops!" I heard.

Harry went pale. He squeezed past and ran into the kitchen. I heard a cry of dismay; "That was my mother's! – It was over a hundred years old!"

There was a murmur of apology; "I'll pay for the damage, Harry – it's time you had a new one anyway if it was that old."

"What's in here?" Greg opened the door Harry had closed a minute ago.

"Wait! – You can't go in there!" Harry fought his way back from the kitchen. But Greg had already gone in, the rest of us trailing behind.

The room, like the hallway, was drab, and hadn't been decorated in a long time. A leather sofa, scuffed, faded, sat at right angles to a high, tiled fireplace, a picture above it. The room was cold but the grate was filled with crumpled newspaper and kindling, a coal scuttle on the hearth. A tiny artificial Christmas tree stood on a cabinet and paper streamers criss-crossed the ceiling. Over near the window was a worn mahogany table, with rolls of coloured wrapping paper, cards, tie-on gift tags, a pair of scissors lying beside them.

And there were toys.

Old toys of wood and tin. Hand-painted, beautifully made – cars, aeroplanes, a drum, a yellow and red puppet with strings, a train set, chipped-edged board games, an army of coloured toy soldiers marching across the table top...

...And over to one side, away from the others, a doll. China, delicate. I glanced down at the gift tags. *To Harold.* Written in a neat unmistakable hand.

There was one, slightly apart from the others. I twisted my head to get a better look. It read: *To Lorna. With Love. Harold.*

I looked round the room again. Looked closer at the picture on the chimney breast; a photograph – two children, a girl and boy, an age difference of two years or so. The boy sat slightly behind the girl, arms round her, protective, bright-eyed both of them, smiling at the camera.

"Please," I heard. "Please go now." Harry stood in the doorway.

"What's all this, then, Harry? Got a secret family, eh?" Greg picked up one of the cars and ran the wheels across the surface of the table. I heard Amy giggle.

"Leave it, Greg," I said. "We'd better go."

But Greg was reaching for the doll. "Who's this for?"

"Don't touch her!" shouted Harry.

But Greg was dragging the doll towards him by one ankle, its dress falling across its face. "Is this one of those dolls that pees?"

Harry lunged towards him and Norman tried to grab him round the waist. Harry broke free, reached across the table and turned, scissors in his hand. Someone, Amy, I think, screamed as Harry went for Greg.

Greg, cowering, stumbled back towards the fireplace, catching his heel, sprawling across the coal scuttle, dropping the doll. Harry stood over him, fingers white round the scissors. "Out! Get out!" He turned to us. "All of you! Get out of my house!"

In the silence that followed I picked up the doll and set it carefully back on the table. Nobody offered to help Greg. He heaved himself up, the battle for dignity long lost, and walked unsteadily out of the room, the back of his coat covered in coal dust.

I was the last to leave. I closed the door behind me and sucked in the cold night air. As we walked down the path, Amy gave a nervous titter.

Greg spoke, voice a little shaky; "Unsociable wee git – Last time I'll visit *him*." He gave a foolish grin, looked round, waiting for somebody to agree but no one said anything.

I got into my car with the other three. I turned the key and the starter gave a whine and died. I tried again and heard a double honk as Greg and

Victor drove away. A hand waved out at us.

Norman and I got out and pushed, Amy behind the wheel. We manoeuvred the car round until it pointed downhill and got back in. I let it roll forward, let out the clutch and sighed with relief when the engine fired. Other than ask Amy to take the wheel I hadn't spoken since we'd left the house.

Near the bottom of the hill Norman said, "Can you imagine a man wrapping up Christmas presents for himself? Kids' toys at that. And a doll? What kind of man does that?" He started to laugh. "What do you think, Andy?"

"I think you're an asshole, Norman."

The inside of the car went silent. I concentrated on the road, white now with frost.

We were a couple of miles along the dual carriageway when I saw the flashing lights ahead of us and slowed to a crawl. The Rover was pulled in at the side, a police car in front of it. Greg was standing trying to steady himself against the bonnet, at the same time blowing into a bag. He turned towards me, not looking at all happy as I edged past.

We came off the dual carriageway and coming up on the first junction when Norman said, "Just drop us off here and we'll get a taxi."

I shrugged, pulled over and they got out and wished Amy a Merry Christmas. They didn't wish me a Merry Christmas. I left them standing there at the edge of the kerb.

I drove in silence to Amy's flat. She was curled up, legs under her, head against my shoulder. She must have gone into a doze for she didn't move until I pulled the car into the kerb. She opened her eyes, lifted her head, drowsy, stretched back against the seat, raised her arms above her head. "Well," she said. "Here we are."

I didn't reply. She moved closer. "Coming up for a cup of coffee?"

"No, thanks," I said.

She giggled. She thought it was funny. I stared out of the windscreen and listened to the splutter of the heater fan. She stopped giggling.

After a minute she moved away from me and fumbled in her handbag. She pulled out her key, opened the door, got out, then swung the door back as far as it would go and slammed it with all her might. The window rattled and something dropped inside the door cavity. She flounced past the bonnet, across the footpath and up the steps and opened the door of her flat.

It must have been almost two o'clock when I turned into the high-hedged road and laboured up the hill. I drove to the top, reversed into an opening and crawled back, stopping the car, pointing downhill.

There was still a chink of light between the curtains. As I went along the path something cold touched my cheek and a flurry of snowflakes drifted down. I pressed the bell push, tried to shrink down into my coat. Almost in an instant the air was thick with falling snow, the silence falling with it.

The transom above me lit up. There was the sound of movement inside.

"Who is it?"

"It's me, Harry…Andy."

"Go away…Leave me alone."

"Let me in, Harry…Please."

"No…Go away. I've got nothing to say to you." The light went out.

I leaned close to the door, snow building on my shoulders. "I'm sorry," I said. I listened and thought I heard a door close somewhere.

I turned and went down the path. The roof of the car was covered in white. I stopped halfway towards the gate and turned. I thought the chink of light between the curtains disappeared for a moment.

"Merry Christmas, Harry," I called softly.

But I don't think he heard me.

I got into the car and the engine fired immediately. I rubbed my forearm across the inside of the windscreen, switched on the wipers, pulled away from the kerb, almost indistinguishable now from the road, and as I rolled quietly down the hill I glanced in the mirror at the twin tracks behind me and wishing I'd taken on the bookies headed for home.

THE SUMMER MY VOICE BROKE

Belfast, 1957

They say she was in on it from the start, the whole made-up thing – the pout, the exaggerated wiggle, the dumb blonde oh-so-slightly-breathless little-girl voice.....

Exams behind us, the school year winding to an end, discipline relaxed nearly to the point of non-existence, the long slow down of days. We should have been sitting in room 11, debating, comparing the styles of Hardy, Trollope, Thackeray…

Where we were was the third row of the stalls of the Imperial Cinema in Cornmarket, the wide Cinemascope screen, De Luxe colour, stretching out to the limits of our vision. "They'll never miss us," Robbie had said.

Robbie. Biggest liar in the school. The thing was we still believed everything he said. No matter how many times he lied to us, we kept on believing him. I mean, take five fellows out of a class of twenty-two and it's hard to imagine how we wouldn't be missed.

"She's got the biggest …" Robbie paused as Mr Dalzell approached, gown flapping like Dracula's cloak.

"Biggest what?" I asked, like I was auditioning for the role of a Tyrolean goat herder. Mr Dalzell was pinning something to the notice board.

"Biggest *what?*" I asked again.

.....She wears a navy suit, cut to accentuate every curve, the front low as decency laws allow, a white rose pinned where the cleavage begins, on her head a wide-brimmed hat the same colour as the suit and she carries a mink stole. Little Richard is belting out the title tune as she sashays down the street. An ice deliveryman is at the tailboard of his truck. His head swivels as she passes and the block of ice in the bed of the truck melts under his hands, the water flowing out under the tailgate. As she turns up a flight of steps to an apartment building a milkman comes out. He stops, gawks, the top bursts off the bottle he is holding, the milk foams over his hand. Inside, she walks along the hall. A man is kneeling at his doorway. He looks up at her and his glasses shatter. And all the while The Sound – raw, rhythmic, like nothing I've ever heard in all of my fifteen years.....

"What was that? What happened just now? – I couldn't make it out." Stanley. I was sitting beside him like I did in the classroom. I was Stanley's eyes. I sat beside him in the middle of the front row of desks, tasked with relaying to him the information on the blackboard while he, nose an inch from his exercise book, copied it out in large black print. His left eye was the worst, the other not much better. It had begun when he was twelve, not long after we started first form. Now, when he looked at you, Stanley turned his head a little to the side, all the better to focus.

I began to give him a running commentary until somebody kicked the back of my seat and a voice told me to for God's sake shut up.

Robbie was on my other side, beyond him Norman and Fitzie. When we had walked into the foyer Robbie had rummaged in his pockets, said he hadn't enough, would I lend him a bob, promising to pay me back the next day. When we sat down I thought I heard a jingle of coins.

Fitzie, whose dad was a bank manager, spoke with a posh accent. All the way into the city centre he wouldn't stop talking about next month's holiday in Portugal. Norman was the quiet one and lived alone with his mother and never mentioned his father.

.....The three Ms. Some people called them "The Big Six". There was Marilyn, of course – everybody knows about Marilyn. Nobody remembers Mamie much.....

We stood in a line on the assembly hall stage.

"Quiet!" shouted Mr Rogers, the noise dying away to the occasional cough and the beat of my heart. He picked up the metre stick.

Unlike the traditional cane a metre stick is not flexible. It was never designed for punishment but had become the weapon of choice for sadists. A cane stings. A metre stick *hurts.*

Robbie was first, which seemed fitting to me.

"Which hand do you write with?" asked Mr Rogers.

"Left." replied Robbie. For once he was telling the truth.

"Left what?"

"Left…Sir."

"Hold out you right hand." Mr Rogers flexed his arm. He seemed at his happiest and you could see anticipation in his washed-out blue eyes. I half expected him to lick his lips. I don't think I ever hated anyone as much.

I was last in line. As he worked his way along the line I prayed his arm would be tired by the time he got to me. He paused a moment before each of them like he was mentally calculating the maximum level of pain he could inflict and still avoid the risk of hospitalisation.

Then it was my turn. "Which hand do you write with?"

"Right…Sir." My voice was a nervous falsetto and someone near the front of the hall sniggered.

He nudged out my other hand with the end of the metre stick. "Hold it straight."

I stretched out my arm and just before closing my eyes saw the beam of sunlight through the tall arched window strike the gold band on his ring finger as the metre stick swept down. It connected with a loud thwop, slightly off angle and something gave in my thumb. I hunched over, holding my hand like a claw.

"Let that be a lesson…and a warning to the rest of you." His eyes panned around the hall before returning to us. "Resume your places." He laid the metre stick reverently on the table and picked up the school hymnal. "This morning's hymn is number one hundred and twenty-six – 'Now thank we all our God, with hands and hearts and voices'." The piano struck up with the opening chord and I followed the others off the stage, cradling my thumb, blinking back the tears, all the while saying to myself; it was worth it…it was worth it……

By the time I got home my thumb was a deep shade of purple. I slipped Flash's collar over his head, clipped on the lead, tried to sneak out again. But I wasn't quick enough. My mother took one look; "What on earth happened to you?"

"Banged it in the woodwork class," I mumbled, my eyes turned away. When I looked back at her she was standing, head cocked, hands on hips, studying my face. Without another word she went to the cupboard and brought out a length of cotton cut from an old bed sheet. She bandaged me up and I took Flash out holding the lead in my good hand.

When my father came home I heard them in quiet discussion out in the hall. "So," he said when he came into the room, undid the bandage and looked at my thumb. "Banged it in woodwork? – I didn't know this was woodwork day." He didn't wait for a response but went out to his tool shed and came back with the bottle of methylated spirits he kept for his blowlamp. He dabbed my thumb and my mother bandaged it up once more.

I never lied to them again.

School year ended and my thumb was slow to heal but with eight weeks of holidays ahead there was much to do – money to make and a guitar to buy. I started with the sale of my toys – my model cars, my train set, my Biggles books. I ran errands, painted gates, chopped wood, cleaned out pigeon lofts. I came to an agreement with a local allotment owner to sell lettuce and trundled round the streets with a wooden crate fitted with a set of pram wheels. By the end of the fourth week I had enough to buy an old guitar with a chipped fretboard and a dent in the sound box. I went to the local library and got out a Bert Weedon instruction manual and retired to my bedroom.

...A small-town girl, married at seventeen, by the time she was twenty-four she'd been on the covers of over five hundred magazines including Life, *under the caption; "Hollywood's Smartest Dumb Blonde". She had gone to the University of Texas, had an IQ over 160, could speak five languages, could play violin.....*

Since early that year my voice had been undergoing change – high one moment, deep the next and various pitches in between – often covering the whole of the octave in a single sentence. Robbie and the others already had manly baritones. Me? I had always been a late developer and was the butt of their jokes and those of my older brother. My mother and father were dismissive of it all and it seemed the only one showing any sympathy was my granddad, my father's father. He lived a mile away and I called with him every Wednesday. When I was leaving he would rest his hand on my shoulder and tell me all the things I wanted to hear.

But the problem was the whole thing was getting in the way of my bid for musical stardom. Furthermore, it turned out that Bert Weedon's guitar manual was fine if all you wanted to sing was Slow Boat To China or She'll Be Comin' Round The Mountain. I decided to make up my own chord sequencing for the songs I wanted to sing, but soon found I had to give up on Good Golly, Miss Molly, as I could no longer be guaranteed that the sustained high-pitched scream necessary for the song would come out high-pitched, or if it did it would remain so. I considered writing to Little Richard to ask if he had ever encountered this problem. As if this wasn't a big enough cross to bear, a cluster of spots had appeared on my chin and no sooner had one gone away than another took its place. I noticed, too, a slight fuzz above my upper lip and hair starting to grow where there had been no hair before.

Robbie's birthday came around and he held a party in his local church hall. Norman was there and Fitzy, who sported a deep suntan and wouldn't stop talking about his fortnight in the Algarve. Stanley didn't come but nobody thought to enquire. I took the opportunity to remind Robbie about the shilling he owed me but he had forgotten to bring any money with him. He introduced me to his older sister, a tall, big-boned girl with a Doris Day hairstyle and an overbite. She shook my hand and said she would see me later.

We had little triangular sandwiches and cake and ice cream and then the tables were pushed back to make room in the centre of the hall. We played Pass the Parcel, Musical Chairs, Blind Man's Buff, and, before we realised, it was ten o'clock and the church caretaker was glaring in, brush in one hand, a paper sack in the other.

"Grand Old Duke of York!" someone shouted. "Yes! – Grand Old Duke of York!" someone else yelled. Everybody started to mill about then, pairing up – a boy and a girl. There seemed to me to be a fair bit of dodging going on. I had heard of the Grand Old Duke of York but wasn't all that familiar with the concept and what would be expected of me. The decision was soon taken out of my hands.

I felt a tug at my sleeve and Robbie's sister stood there, smiling coyly. She grabbed me firmly by the arm and led me to where the others were lining up in pairs as though preparing to board the Ark. The gramophone started up, a marching tune, and everyone began to sing; "The Grand Old Duke of York….He had ten thousand men…" What had, until then, been a lacklustre evening was about to change.

The couple at the front of the line stopped and turned to face each other, hands clasped, held high, forming an arch. The other couples tramped forward, ducking under. Then, without any warning, the music stopped. The two forming the arch dropped their arms entrapping the couple passing through. Everybody cheered and the boy leaned forward and kissed his more-than-willing partner. The arms were raised, the music started again and the line of couples moved forward.

As the beads of sweat broke on my forehead Robbie's sister turned, nudged me and gave me a close-up of her overbite and in that instant I knew she'd been round the Grand Old Duke of York circuit – and a block or two – before.

The boy behind dug me in the back and I lurched forward. As we circled round the hall and entered the kissing zone I quickened my pace, the music stopped and the pair behind got caught.

Fourth time round it happened. As I went to duck under, the arms came down – slightly ahead of the pause in the music I was convinced, but all hope deserted me. A pair of strong hands hauled me round. I looked frantically about but I hadn't a chance. Robbie's sister's arms encircled my neck, cutting off any hope of escape and the flow of blood through my carotid artery. She came at me like a conger eel. Her overbite prised open my lips and I felt my oxygen supply being sucked away. It seemed to go on forever and just as my legs began to buckle, mercifully it was over and the boy behind was shoving me again.

I staggered off to the side and stood there, whooping for air. Robbie's sister leaned in close and spoke into my ear; "See you around, big boy." And she walked off to where a group of other girls stood, all of them hunched over in fits of laughter.

My grandfather died three days later.

I came home from my lettuce round to find my father at home, dressed in his good suit. My mother was out, he said, buying a cardigan. And then he told me. He seemed to have difficulty getting the words out and then he turned away and stood looking out of the window, his back to me, head down, shoulders starting to shake.

I had never seen him like this before and I didn't know what to do. So I said the only thing that came to mind. I told him I'd take Flash for a walk.

.....She was once interviewed by a television presenter. He asked her; "Is it true you walked down Sunset Boulevard with a tiger on a pink lead?" "Yes," she replied. "I like pink."......

By now I had seen the film several times as it moved out through the suburban cinemas before ending its run. I never tired of it. I sat alone in the dark, anticipating every guitar riff, every staccato drumbeat, every saxophone moan. And in the times between I would sit on the edge of my bed, practising chord changes, tapping out the beat with my foot on the cool linoleum floor.

On an early September morning I crawled out of bed, crossed to the window and pulled back the curtains. There was a film of mist on the windscreen of Mr Walker's old Morris. I went into the bathroom and stood in front of the mirror. My spots didn't seem quite so bad. I looked at my brother's electric razor lying on the shelf…

When I went downstairs and spoke to my mother my voice was low and steady. I ate my breakfast, slipped on my school blazer, slung my bag over my shoulder and walked to the bus stop with a sudden confidence and a realisation that the seasons were moving on and my life with them.

The Imperial Cinema is long gone and a shoe shop stands on the site. Robbie became a missionary and the last I heard he was somewhere in Papua New Guinea. He still owes me a shilling. Stanley never returned to school. His eyesight deteriorated so quickly his parents withdrew him on medical advice and I heard he finished his education with a home tutor.

I never saw him again. Norman was killed when the single engine of the light aircraft he was flying failed and he crashed into a hillside in Cumbria. Fitzie is currently serving a two-year sentence for fraud.

I saw him once, years on, frail, washed-out blue eyes dulled by time.

I was stepping out of the lift at the insurance office where I worked. As the doors parted he was standing there. He seemed a little confused, looking about him. I hesitated, considered walking on. Instead I asked if I could help.

"I'm looking for the claims department," he said. "I want to report something lost – a ring."

.....and just before closing my eyes saw the beam of sunlight through the tall arched window strike the gold band on his ring finger as the metre stick swept down.....

I looked at his hand. There was a furrow on his finger where the ring had been. "My wife gave it to me – a long time ago." His voice faltered.

I told him I'd show him the way and he followed me back inside the lift. We rode up to the fourth floor in silence apart from a brief comment on the weather. The lift slid open and I pointed to the door of the claims department. He thanked me and walked stiffly towards it. When he had gone a few paces I called after him; "I was one of your pupils."

He turned. "Were you? Were you, really?" He squinted at me. There was a moment of silence while we looked at one another. "Did I ever....?" He stopped, blinked, lowered his head.

"Yes," I said. "Once."

He was an old man, unable to look me in the eye. He started to say something; "I'm so..." but the rest got lost in the lurch and rumble of the lift doors as they slid together.

I stood there a moment staring at the panel inches from my face, things unfinished on the other side. Then I pressed the down button, aware, suddenly, that I was cradling my left thumb.

.....She died in 1967 when the car she was travelling in hit the back of a lorry outside New Orleans as she was on her way to a television studio. They say she was decapitated. Others say this was an urban myth and what people saw was her blonde wig. She was thirty-four years old.....

That summer a Prime Minister told us we'd never had it so good. Here, a portent of things to come, a policeman was killed in a booby-trap explosion. Oliver Hardy died and Jimmy Greaves signed for Chelsea. There was some fantasy talk of a tunnel under the sea between England and France. A bomb was tested on an island on the far side of the world and I felt a moment of fear. I learnt to play guitar and had my first kiss and decided, for the time being anyhow, that learning guitar was safer. I lied to my mother. An old man died and I saw my father cry. I put away childish things.

It's strange, but I seem only to remember Robbie and the others through a clear association with that summer and not for all those times before and up until we left school and, in the progression of things, went our separate ways. Even now, when I go to a birthday party I check around for big girls with overbites. My grandfather, that kind old man, is the fondest of memories and I still sometimes sense his hand on my shoulder and this... this more than anything... At the rare mention of her name I see her in an instant, walking across that wide cinema screen while the block of ice melts and in my head I hear again that sound: the fusion of chords and rhythm – raucous rebellious, heavy on the backbeat, and I smile to myself in the quiet and certain knowledge that it was all only rock 'n' roll.

WHERE THE DEER AND
THE ANTELOPE PLAY

Belfast, 1952, 2002

In the dream the man, red-whiskered face, pushes himself up from the track, stretches over the edge of the platform and snatches his ankle. He screams and tries to pull free but the man's grip is too strong. He twists round, shouting to Jimmy, "Help me! Help me!" But Jimmy isn't there anymore. The man is standing now, other hand reaching for him. His face is mottled, even in the gloom David knows this, and there is blood trickling from his ears. David screams again, "Somebody help me!".....

That is the dream. In the waking world the man was small, thin, gaunt grey face and he didn't rise from the track. He lay there, outstretched arm twitching and coming to rest half over the wooden sleeper. The blood was real.

The morning air was clear, September crisp, the wind tugging at his upturned collar. He walked the way a stranger would along the tarmac path, the roofs of the houses just visible beyond the raised banking on either side. The conservation volunteers had done their best to tidy the verges but it was a losing battle against the dog faeces and beer cans and fast food cartons.

He looked for a marker of some sort, something out of memory, but the area had been long since redeveloped and the new housing didn't help, rises levelled out, straight stretches curved, everything changed.

He heard the whirr of approaching wheels and stepped to one side. The cyclist passed – grey helmet, skin-tight top, three-quarter-length lycra trousers – head down, legs pumping, breathing hard, records to beat. Further along, beyond the cyclist, a young couple pushed a child in a pedal car.

His eyes scanned the left bank, heavy with whin bushes and other growth he couldn't name. He slowed, turning one way then the other. Here…somewhere about here…

Then he saw it – almost totally obscured by the greens and yellows of wildflower and tall weed. He went over, reached out, pulled aside the growth, exposing the concrete edge, bits broken off here and there. There was only a short section intact, covered in lichen. Just under four feet in height it had seemed much higher then when the two boys…..

…..squeezed through the gap in the corrugated fence, Jimmy reaching into his pocket, pulling out the packet of cigarettes. David's mother, no reason given, had voiced disapproval of the friendship that had developed between them, but David had fallen a little under the spell of the older boy with his smart tongue and persuasive ways.

They had met up as planned at the rear of the old doctor's house, long since uninhabited, the windows boarded up, the old story, often told, of the murder, many years ago, of a young girl, her bloody handprint on the wall re-appearing time and again with each vain attempt to cover it with paint.

It was early April, not quite dark, as they made their way along the path towards the track. It had been over a year since the last train on the line and the weeds had taken hold, the windows on the station house broken, the door hanging from its hinges. David switched on his torch, a birthday present, pocket-size, gold-lacquered, battery a little weak.

They weren't expecting anyone else to be there and when the man appeared in the torch's beam he was as startled as they were. It all happened so quickly. He leapt up and rushed towards them, the boys recoiling from the doorway, the torch spinning from David's hand. The man, small, thin, in an old oversize gabardine coat, collided with Jimmy and Jimmy pushed him away, the man reeling towards David.

It wasn't intentional at the start. It wasn't intentional at all. David fended off the man who again lurched towards Jimmy. Jimmy giggled and shoved and then it was David's turn once more – and that was when the madness took over. Back and forth the man stumbled, David starting to feel the power, Jimmy shoving a little harder each time, the pair of them laughing now. The man tried to get away from them but Jimmy blocked his way, spinning him round, sending him back towards David, the man losing balance and reeling on by.

Later, replaying it in his head – forever replaying it in his head – David realised what was about to happen, the man moving too fast, unable to stop, momentum taking him towards the platform edge. His shoes lost their grip on the smooth concrete and arms flailing, clawing at the air and with a low wail, the only noise he'd made throughout, he skidded feet first off the platform. There was a sound, unlike any sound David had ever heard as the back of the man's head hit the concrete edge.

The two boys, breathing hard, stared at one another. It was Jimmy who moved first. He went over to the platform edge, David behind him. The man lay face up, one leg bent under him, the other stretched across the metal rail. David peered down into the gloom, looking for signs of movement, but there weren't any. He swallowed, his throat gone dry. "What are we going to do?"

"Run!" said Jimmy. He pulled at David's sleeve. "It was an accident! Come on!"

"No! We can't! – We can't just leave him like that!"

"Yes, we can! Come on! We need to get out of here!"

"But he's hurt! We can maybe help him!"

"Well, you can stay if you want! – I'm not!" Jimmy backed away. "It was an accident," he said again. He broke into a run back along the path in the direction of the main road.

David stared down at the man lying across the track. There was a dark pool of something forming close to one of his ears. He started to cry. He looked after Jimmy, racing towards the gap in the fence, took one more look at the man, turned and ran.

When he got home he paused outside for a moment, brushing his hands over his clothes. He took several deep breaths. Should I tell them? They're bound to suspect something – soon as they see me they'll know something's wrong. What should I do? It was an accident, wasn't it?... Wasn't it?

He opened the door quietly, slipped into the narrow hall. The living-room door was closed and he could hear the radio – Big Bill Campbell and The Rocky Mountain Boys, a strong baritone – *Oh, give me a home where the buffalo roam...* He eased the door closed, slid the bolt across, moved to the foot of the stairs, stepping over the creaky third tread, the singing fainter; *...and the skies are not cloudy all day...*

It was then he remembered the torch.

It was mid-morning the following day, a Saturday, when word started to spread round the neighbourhood; an early-morning dog walker had found a man lying dead on the old railway line, the police knocking on doors, asking questions. David stood near the back of the bystanders. He couldn't see Jimmy anywhere and the mid-day news merely referred to a man found dead on the old railway track. The word from the police was there was no indication of suspicious circumstances.

The evening paper didn't add anything – big headline, little story content – a man, as yet unidentified and thought to be homeless, had been found on the disused railway line close to the old station house. He was believed to have been sleeping there. It was thought that at some time during the night he wandered out and in the darkness missed his footing, striking his head on the platform edge. A half-empty bottle of methylated spirits was discovered nearby.

The week-end passed and no more information came out. It was the talk of the neighbourhood for a while, but come Monday it was old news and other news had taken its place.

He didn't speak to Jimmy the following week. He tried to avoid him as far as possible, as though by doing so he could convince himself the whole thing had never happened. One morning their eyes met across the school playground and Jimmy's eyes said; "Don't tell...Don't ever tell."

And he never did.

The weeks went by and the weeks turned into months and he didn't see Jimmy after that. The word at school was that Jimmy's father had got a new job and the family had moved away. David's mother made it clear that it was no loss, she'd heard things about Jimmy's family but she wouldn't say what they were.

It wasn't long before David's schoolwork deteriorated. His end-of-term exam results were poor. Where he had been a normal, good-natured, popular teenager he became surly, morose, answered back to his parents. In the end he broke another pupil's nose in a playground fight and got expelled on the spot.

He tried to get a job but when they heard about the incident in school they turned him away. He managed to pick up a little unskilled work here and there over the next couple of years and as soon as he was old enough he joined the army. When his training finished his unit was posted to Germany. He married a German girl when he was twenty-one, separated at twenty-three, divorced at twenty-four, a daughter somewhere. On leaving the army he drifted from place to place and when he was close to forty years of age his father died and he came home. His army career had been without blemish and he got a job with an engineering company, making moulds for machinery parts, shift work mostly. He worked hard, kept himself to himself, didn't complain and was considered an oddball by his fellow workers. He met a woman in a bar one night, married her within six months, separated two years later. He got caught up on the fringe of the paramilitaries and was taken in a few times for questioning. His mother died. The engineering company went into liquidation and he was jobless once again.

From time to time he would read about Jimmy Golightly, see the photographs in the papers – Jimmy getting elected onto the local council, Jimmy shaking hands with a visiting dignitary, Jimmy sitting at a low table with nursery children, Jimmy firing the starting pistol at a charity run…

And throughout it all, the dream – the red-whiskered face, the man reaching over the edge of his memory, handprints on a wall.

He remembered the good times before this present life. He remembered when he was a boy travelling in the train to the coastal town with his mother and father, the journey through fields of wheat and hay and potato, over rivers and roads, the high railway banks, the hedges, the telephone wires undulating in synchrony to the sound of the track rods. He remembered the lurch and sway of the carriage, the creak of springs, the leather smell of the door strap, the guillotine drop of the window, the rush of air. He remembered, in his boyhood imagination, the passing countryside turning into panoramic plain, the grazing sheep wild deer, the cows vast roaming herds of buffalo as far as the eye could see. He remembered fighting off the whooping hordes of Apache, knocking them one by one off their ponies with a well-aimed finger, till they were all gone and he and his mother and his father were safe once more......

On an early November night when he was 64 years old David Lamb walked towards his home. A fog was dropping down and his chest hurt a little with each inward breath, his eyes teary with the chill. Home was a top-floor flat in a row of old Edwardian terraced houses in the outer north of the city. He was not long finished work on the late shift, stacking shelves in the supermarket and he had thought about picking up a take-away, but the queue was longer than he would have liked.

He turned into the street where he lived, quiet now but not always so. He would have preferred to be somewhere else but the rent was as much as he could afford.

At first he didn't pay a lot of attention to the car parked ahead of him but as he walked past the engine started. He had only gone a few more paces when he became aware it was keeping abreast of him. Then it moved ahead a little and came to a stop. He slowed his pace. Things had got a lot better in the past few years but for him the old fears and instincts would never go away.

As he drew level with the car the front-passenger window slid down. "Hello, David."

In another time he would have turned, run back the way he had come. Instead he leaned down, looked inside, trying to make out the figure behind the wheel. It didn't take long. He hadn't seen any photographs in recent times – no dinner-suited functions, no unveiling of plaques, no cutting of ribbons. David didn't say anything, just stood there. "Get in, David – I won't bite, I promise," said Jimmy Golightly.

David hesitated, reached for the handle and opened the door. The interior of the car smelt faintly of air freshener. He lowered himself onto the seat. He didn't say anything, thinking; Why? Why now after so many years?

He closed the door, the courtesy light gently dying. "How'd you find me?"

"There are ways. It took a while – best part of six months, in fact." replied Jimmy. The fog drifted round a street lamp, visibility diminishing, the uncertainty of colours. A group of youths, four of them, passed the car, crossing the road, one grabbing another in a neck hold, wrestling him past the lamppost, shouting, the other breaking free, thrusting his fingers up in the V sign.

"Why?" asked David. "Why, now … after all this time?"

Jimmy didn't answer. He fumbled in the door pocket and set something on David's lap. A plastic bag. David looked at the bag then at Jimmy. Jimmy nodded down. David felt inside – a cylindrical shape, fluted at one end. "Batteries can be a problem – they're a different size nowadays," said Jimmy. He lifted a pack of cigarettes from the dashboard and offered one to David. David shook his head.

He brought out the torch from the bag. In the street-light glow he could see the gold lacquer peeling in places, a dent near the switch.

"You had this all along?"

Jimmy was slow to answer. "I went back. Later … after it got dark… I went back. I trod on it … That's why it's dented."

"Why are you doing this? Why, after all these years?"

The fog cleared for an instant and a hundred yards ahead of them a bus pulled in, the four youths sprinting towards it, still shouting, pushing one another.

"Look at me and tell me what you see."

David turned towards the man beside him. Jimmy's eyes met his – a haunted look and David knew now why there had been no photographs in the papers in recent times, no write-ups. He turned away again. After a while he said, "How long?"

"I've seen my last summer," said Jimmy. He blew smoke out of the partly-open window and looked down at his cigarette. He held it up between finger and thumb, examined it closely. "Ironic, isn't it?" David didn't say anything. After a moment Jimmy asked, "Did you ever tell anyone?"

"No – Nobody."

"Some secret to carry with you all your life, right?" Suddenly Jimmy's head went down, the cigarette burning forgotten in his finger tips. There was a long silence in the car. When he spoke again it was little more than a whisper; "It was an accident... Wasn't it?"

He was surprised to find the old house still there. From where he had been standing on the walkway it was hidden from view by almost fifty years of tree growth and it was only when he came level with the entrance path he saw it. For some reason he had expected it to have been long since demolished, replaced by something more modern. The brickwork had been re-pointed, the window mouldings recently painted, a serviceable mid-grey, an extension jutting out at the rear.

Curiosity took him up the short path to the front door. There was a brass plaque at one side – The Golightly Centre, in clear, unfussy lettering.

He opened the door and stepped inside. He was in a smallish reception area, simply furnished, a desk in front of the far wall. There was no one about, music playing somewhere, easy listening.

He looked round him. There were several pictures on the walls, one of them a portrait of Jimmy. He went over. It was a good likeness, a Jimmy in earlier days. Below it hung a smaller framed photograph – Jimmy, clearly unwell now, a large key in his hand, posing at the front door of the building with half a dozen other people.

"Can I help you?" He swung round. He hadn't heard the woman approach. Late fifties, tall.

"No...I...I used to live near here...I remember this house..." He hesitated. "It was a long time ago...I was just a kid. It had been a doctor's house and then it lay empty for years...I thought it would have been knocked down by now." He tried to summon up a smile; "It was supposed to be haunted."

The woman smiled back. "I heard about that, but there are no ghosts here. I doubt if there's a town in the western world that doesn't lay claim to that story." She had a wholesome face, light brown hair, flecks of white. "It's a shelter for the homeless now – thanks to him." She nodded towards the painting. David looked at it again and his eyes drifted to the photograph – the woman standing slightly behind and to Jimmy's left. He looked round at her, the hair shorter now, a different style. She saw the expression on his face and nodded. "My husband. He died a little while ago..." She seemed to lose her composure for a moment, fought to regain it. "He campaigned for such a long time for this place. Talked about it from

174

when we first met. His dream, I suppose. He said – when he first became ill – that there were only two things he needed to do before he died. One of them was to see this shelter opened…He never told us what the other was…" She lapsed into silence for a moment, then; "You were studying him very closely…as if you were looking for something. I almost got the impression…" She paused; "Did you know him?"

…the man, red-whiskered face, pushes himself up from the track, stretches over the edge of the platform and snatches his ankle. He screams and tries to pull free but the man's grip is too strong. He twists round, shouting to Jimmy: "Help me! Help me! But Jimmy isn't there anymore…

David looked up at the portrait. "No…I didn't know him …I didn't know him at all."

He retraced his path along the walkway in the direction of the old viaduct. A boy in a school uniform was coming towards him. He recognised the blazer and tie of his old school all those years ago. The colours were the same but the badge was a different design. As the distance between them shortened David studied the boy closely, unsure what he was looking for, trying to find some reminder of the way he used to be. The boy's face took on a wary expression and he quickened his step, moving well to one side as they passed one another.

He walked on, head down, collar raised, sensing the boy turning and looking back. Ahead of him, the path curved to the left taking him in the direction of the main road. The September breeze rustled through the bushes on either side and for a moment he thought he heard something else: old sounds from another life – the hiss of steam, the rhythm of wheels, the thunder of hooves.